# The Doorkeeper

By Octavius Pitt

Published in 2008 by YouWriteOn.com

First Edition

Published by YouWriteOn.com

# THE DOORKEEPER

## Chapter One

For he comes, the human child
To the waters and the wild
With a faerie hand in hand
For the world's more full of weeping
Than you can understand.
W. B. Yates

I am the Doorkeeper. Drysorion as the Welsh of old called me. Mad Silas. I am timeless as are the many other keepers across this beautiful planet. Our duty is to take a few chosen human beings across the void, to a time before time. The world was young in that newborn age and humanity came to understand that the planet was alive in the same sense that they were alive; a living creature with a great soul. The people called the planet's soul, Mother Earth. And they realised She was watching over them with concern. She remains the same today; a creature like you, but mighty beyond your measure. The world beneath your feet is Her body. Her soul lives within it, as your soul lives within your body. Those first people grew civilisations in harmony with Mother Earth and gained great benefit from them. Yet humanity perished through its own mistakes and the Earth moved on through time and space. All this I saw, because I exist as long as She does.

A Doorkeeper is part of Mother Earth's fabric, a life-force to do Her bidding. My knowledge through Her is vast. It told me an exceptional child was coming to this land of Wales. I made ready for him because She knew and deemed him special. Perhaps he was to be a messenger or an ambassador? Maybe a tool to correct your foolish abuse of the Earth which gains momentum with each passing year? Not every correction succeeds, and Mother Earth has paid the penalty over many thousands of years. She is patient; but has limits to Her patience and your pollution and ignorance are once more begging of Her to intervene. But we will see... All moments are mine and I will wait.

\*     \*     \*

In a beautiful house in southern England fear and greed wreck a titled English family, changing those individuals forever.

25 April 1931

Lady Siân Webster looked through the leaded light window of her beautifully appointed dining room with sharp-eyed attention, her stomach was trying to turn somersaults but she held it down. Daylight had begun to fade across Pampisford Road and the fields beyond, vehicles with their lights bright were moving like toys along the Purley Way. Fear clawed icily at her back but she held that down too, her lovely hazel eyes scrutinising distant Croydon Airport with good reason.

'Daddy's home!'

A little Austin Seven pulled up outside the front gate with a squeal from its big, narrow tyres; her son, who was playing outside shouted again from the paved driveway. Lord Webster thanked the driver for his lift home, climbed out and walked across the pavement to be confronted by the excited ten-year-old. The briefcase fell and James, dark eyed and slim, dressed in an immaculate, expensive business suit opened his arms wide. His natural aristocratic elegance vanished in seconds as he whirled Jonathan around to mutual shrieks of glee. Siân felt her insides shred as she watched her husband drop his briefcase to the ground, and open his arms. It was the way he crouched down to scoop the boy up, swinging him round and hugging him with genuine adoration. If only she could feel that way.

'Mrs Eldridge has your dinner ready.' Siân stood at the bottom of the stairs, composed, beautiful, her manicured fingers smoothing the sharply pleated skirt. In spite of her aristocratic husband's air flight home from Italy, via France, she had nothing else to say and walked through to the lounge. Her name, pronounced Sharn, and meaning Jane in English, was the only vestige of her Welsh upbringing she had allowed into her new life.

Later, he was in his pleasant study off the spacious hall, sitting at an escritoire and sifting paperwork when she opened the door and closed it behind like the priming click of a bomb. For many years emotions had been kept in check. Reason triumphing over emotion – it had got her where she wanted to be. But the dam was once again near to bursting. On rare occasions Siân allowed herself to remember her origins and childhood home which had been harsh, unglamorous and certainly rustic as little more than a rural sewer. To call her memory of it prejudiced would be an understatement.

4

Etiquette, self taught by tattered books in a small candle lit room after a fourteen hour day in service was the chosen norm. She watched everything; hearing her upper class employer's diction, that of their friends, business associates and servants; of new ideas and heady aspirations. The benefit of a shrewd mind armed little Siân Williams with her own harsh ambition and at sixteen years of age it set her towards the goal she considered as betterment. Such was the total overthrow of the staid, straitjacket of Edwardian society at the end of World War One that in three years, through cunning and physical beauty, Siân had won the heart of a young, war-shattered baronet who came home to many dead and scattered relatives. Therein lay her chance for a new life she could only dream of.

Her charm was natural; her knowledge of books, music and culture self-taught. An ability to hold her tongue in demanding circumstances was near total through self-will and the young James Ashbourne Webster learned, after his society wedding, in slow, startling increments about the sea of passion which ebbed and flowed beneath his new wife's wonderful veneer.

All the acquired middle-class elegance, panache, crème de la crème that had seemed to everyone the essence of an aristocrat-by-marriage, dissolved into vitriolic bile in that moment James turned to look at her. Their desperate financial situation had turned a key, opening a dark secret door into Siân's own personal hell of poverty and destitution. For the first time in their eleven year marriage she was about to fall a thousand miles beneath the epitome of an aristocrat's wife. The stunning Welsh beauty who had married the twenty-year-old son of a soon to be dead English lord, was about to reveal her long suppressed terror in one moment of weakness.

Jonathan walked from his bedroom onto the landing dressed in blue stripped pyjamas with Mr Chips, his teddy bear cuddled to his chest and sat down, legs dangling through the spindles of the balustrade.

'You're having an affair with that newspaper tart aren't you? You've never satisfied me in your entire life and you'll never satisfy her...'

James' lean-handsome, hungry countenance remained quiet and still as his dark, determined eyes fastened on his wife's twisted features. Her clever, desperate tongue found more and more invectives to hurl; double-dealing, disgust at his failure as a breadwinner and man. The English lord opened his briefcase and took out a sheaf of papers. He laid them face down on the leather top of the escritoire without speaking; much to her astonishment, for James was not a weakling. Siân stood in silence, looking at her husband who flicked through a small leather address book, lifted the earpiece from the telephone and dialled a number.

'Hello. Felicity? James Webster.' He paused. 'Yes we're fine, thank you. Could I speak to Paul, please?'

The voice at the other end went quiet and a deeper voice crackled his name.

'Yes. Hello, Paul...'

Siân lifted her wide eyes and moved closer to the telephone.

'...I need an urgent talk with your department.'

'Is this connected with the country you've just returned from?'

Webster's lips were thin and tight as he gave affirmation.

'And its leader?'

'Yes.'

'OK. I will make the arrangements! Love to Siân and Jonathan.'
The line went dead.

### 29 April 1931

Lady Webster was approaching her luxurious secret hideaway in Warwick Way, Central London feeling uneasy. She was dressed in an immaculate fine silk dress and loose velvet jacket. A fashionable leather bag full of parcels wrapped in Harrods paper was on her arm with a chic new crocodile skin handbag by Ludovic in her hand.

It was a lovely evening, full of high broken cloud, though the day had started with rain. Siân was within ten minutes of her new apartment, not far from Vauxhall Bridge as the sun broke through and her attention was drawn to a tall man who crossed the road by Victoria Station. He wore a gabardine raincoat and fedora; as they walked she gained the distinct impression that he was following her. She entered the lobby of her apartment building, watching with wary eyes from the shadows as he passed by. Forced bravery had kept her in the lobby and as the apartment door closed behind her, uneasiness turned to fear. From behind ruffled chintz curtains Lady Webster scanned the street below - everything looked quite normal. She took a decanter from a tall chiffonier, her heart pounding crazily, found a glass and swallowed a large malt; this calmed frazzled nerves for a while, but the uneasy feeling returned. She sat down in an easy chair feeling like a wet rag and remembered no more until waking two hours later.

Outside, early evening had given way to a clear night and in the near darkness her hazel eyes shone with sudden, obdurate fear. She had no regard for the dire plight of her husband who was at that moment less than two miles away in Shaftesbury Avenue, searching for her in desperation and trying to hang on to the last vestiges of their marriage and financial life. James' problems were of little matter. She had moved on and had to see this adventure through. A pack of Passing Cloud was found in her new handbag and in spite of only smoking for effect, she fumbled a cigarette to her lips.

Early the previous morning, Siân had left an unemotional farewell note to her husband on the dining table, their tearful ten-year-old son looking on in wide-eyed astonishment whilst clutching the hand of their housekeeper. Not long afterwards she caught a London bound commuter train from Croydon East station, walking out on her family with a single-minded determination that was as cool as it was precise.

Siân looked at her watch and her heart leapt. A well-built man had stepped out of a taxicab and entered the lobby below. David wasn't due for another hour. What was he doing? Perhaps something had gone wrong? She crushed the thought: David Templeman was far too self-possessed to let anything go wrong.

The gold-edged light switch clicked to her manicured fingers and Lord Webster's unfaithful wife prepared herself for the man who had guaranteed a life rich beyond unspoken dreams, or her wild imaginings.

Lady Webster would not see, touch or hold Jonathan in her arms for the rest of her life; although he would see her and what she was to become in the most remarkable way. Already the boy was established onto a wild and curious path through the intervention of a spiritual entity called, Doorkeeper. This being he would confront one day.

# Two

## 22 May 1931 - London, England

'Telephone me, please darling.' Eleanor Capenhurst dipped a slim hand into her handbag and lifted out her gold-edged calling card. She presented it with a relaxed smile to the handsome young man who had escorted her home from a chic party.

The door behind opened and together they turned in surprise. A middle-aged man stood in the doorway of her sumptuous apartment with Eleanor's uniformed French maid looking over his shoulder in bewilderment.

'Ah, Mrs Capenhurst.' The man glared through large, round wire-framed glasses and did up the belt of his light coat with theatrical affectation before continuing. 'I have left a message with your maid. The gist of it is that Jonathan seems to be refusing any form of educational activity at the moment and I can no longer undertake the arduous task of teaching him!' The tutor managed a scornful sniff, Eleanor stepped back somewhat bemused as he stepped out onto the landing.

'My account will be in the post.' He proffered a neat brown trilby hat and made his way past them at speed and down the stairs.

'I'm sorry, madam. Master Jonathan and Monsieur 'Arris did not seem to like each other very much. Your nephew threw 'is afternoon lemonade at Monsieur 'Arris -.'

They looked down the stairs at a large wet patch on the collar and back of the tutor's coat as he disappeared into the first floor stairwell.

'Oh my God...'

'I'd best be going then?'

She turned, her face changing from bleak anger to a brief smile. 'Would you mind, Norman...not the best of occasions.'

'I'll 'phone Saturday evening, say six-thirty?'

'Saturday week...'

He nodded acquiescence and turned down the stair with downhearted pace.

Jonathan was not in the huge lounge. Eleanor turned to her maid. 'What happened, Jeannette? Tell me slowly, why did Mr Harris get so upset?'

The girl bobbed a curtsey. She was a pretty twenty-year-old with a turned up nose and short, dark shiny hair. 'Sorry, madam. I was in your room putting your evening dress away an' cleaning, so I did not 'ear anything until I came out. Monsieur 'Arris 'ad 'is coat on and was calling out for me. Then Master Jonathan threw 'is sandwich at 'im.' She broke into a sudden, smothered giggle and stumbled into apologies before realising that her mistress was smiling merrily.

'What happened next?'

'I must have gasped out loud because Monsieur 'Arris looked round at me and then Master Jonathan picked up 'is lemonade and threw that as well. Monsieur 'Arris, 'e was very angry. "E was all wet an' say that 'e never come back.'

Eleanor turned away for a moment, near to stupid laughter. She regained herself enough for propriety. 'I want a pot of tea for me, a tray with cake, biscuits and another glass of lemonade for Master Jonathan.' She put her grey cashmere coat on the back of an elegant Georgian couch in front of huge latticed picture windows that overlooked the metropolis outside, and walked across to a corridor which led to three bedrooms. The boy's sobs could be heard from the first. Eleanor knocked on the white door. 'Jonathan?'

The sobbing stopped immediately.

She entered and saw him lying on the bed, face buried into a big feather pillow. The boy cocked a wary eye out, saw his aunt enter the room and come up to the bed.

'Why has Mr Harris left, Jonathan?

He did not reply and from the protection of his feather pillow watched her pull up a chair to the side of his bed.

'I'm going to sit here until you tell me. And the longer I sit here, the angrier I'm going to get - so I suggest you tell me now!'

The boy sat up, propped himself against the carved bed head and glared at the wall.

'You are an absolute disgrace, Jonathan Webster. When I left this morning you were perfectly turned out - how on earth did you get into that state?' She made an effort to lower her voice. 'And whatever happened to Mr Harris?

'I hate him.' Jonathan turned to her, dark eyes red furious. 'And I hate you!'

'Why?'

'Because I do.'

Eleanor picked up her handbag, took out a cigarette case and put it back. She sat looking at him, lost for words.

'Your shoes should not be on that clean bed!'

He pulled the shoes off and threw them one after the other against the wall with force.

Eleanor lost her temper. She grabbed hold of his hand, pulled it up and smacked his arm as hard as she could. He howled indignation, rolled over and buried himself back into his feather pillow. Eleanor shook her hand which was stinging a great deal and sat down. They said nothing else to each other until a careful knock came to the bedroom door.

'Tea's ready, madam.'

'Thank you, Jeannette. We'll be right out.

'Come on young man. You and I are going to sit out in the lounge and have a long talk...' She pulled on his arm, he resisted and Eleanor threatened him with another smack.

The maid kept out of the way as they came out, although the lounge was due to be cleaned. She had prepared what was almost a high tea from a goodly supply of food in the larder; a beautiful cake with fresh cream, biscuits, a jug of fresh lemonade and a pot of tea.

The boy sat before his aunt at a large Emile Gallé art nouveau table in the middle of the room, as if about to receive the last rights before execution.

'Jonathan, your father asked me to look after you until he returns from America. It shouldn't be long.' She patted his hand. 'We both know you must continue your education.' She poured a glass of lemonade and put it before the boy. 'Why could you not work for Mr Harris?'

'I want to go to my old school.'

Eleanor nodded. 'Yes. I do understand that, but Croydon is much too far to travel each day. You can see that can't you?'

He looked up and said nothing.

'Drink your lemonade.' Eleanor smiled, her dark Webster family eyes sparkled, easing the tension between them just a little. 'Cake?'

The boy took a huge slice and started eating with a pastry fork as he was obliged to do. He drank some of his lemonade and looked at his aunt, sudden determination in his face. 'I hate Finsbury Park. I want to live with my grandmother and grandfather.'

'But they have been dead for years, darling.'

'No. My other ones - in Wales.'

'On your mother's side?'

He nodded, cream around his mouth.

Eleanor sighed, looked at the cup of tea she had poured, and took a sip. 'But I've never met them, sweetheart - and nor have you. Why on earth would you want to go and live all the way up there?'

Jonathan looked out of the window. The busy pace of London was evident in the otherwise silent room.

'Mother has left. Dad is in America. I've got no mother or father any more. No one at all. No one real - you're not real...'

Eleanor looked puzzled, not hurt. 'Why am I not real, Jonathan?'

The boy's face dropped a little and he looked ashamed. 'You're a lady. A proper lady I mean - rich. You're not real. I want a real family like Arthur Sanders and Fred Plummer.' He looked at her, total honesty in his young face.

'But we don't know your grandparents address or even if they are still alive?'

He wiped his sticky hands on a napkin and pulled out something from his back pocket, holding it to his chest in distrust. 'You won't be angry with me, Aunt Eleanor?'

'Why?' She looked puzzled.

'I stole it.'

'Stole what?'

'This.' Jonathan put a crumpled letter on to the table. It sat before them, captive with the silence. She didn't touch it.

'Stole a letter?'

He nodded.

'From whom?'

'Mother. She was packing her things after Dad went up to London.' He took a gulp at his lemonade and burst into tears. Eleanor sat without demur and after a while the boy continued between sobs. 'She had clothes, papers and things and was putting them into her big bag. The letter fell on the floor and when she carried the bag out to the hall I picked it up.'

'Why didn't you give your mother the letter, Jonathan?'

'She was leaving me. She said she would send for me when she could. I was scared, Aunt Eleanor.' He slurped more lemonade. 'I wanted to have something of hers,' he looked across the table in pleading, 'in case she never came back...'

Eleanor felt a lump in her throat as the boy ran from the room crying fitfully. She sat for some moments and picked up the letter. It was old; the faint post mark confirmed the fact, giving a date of June 1917. She finished her cup of tea, poured herself another and took out the faded letter. It was from Siân to her mother and father in Wales and

12

written a few weeks after she had left home to start work as an under parlour maid at a doctor's house in Belgravia Square, London. Fascinated, Eleanor read on with genuine astonishment; her wildest dreams could not have placed Lady Siân Webster in service – it seemed impossible.

Siân would acknowledge being born in Wales, but did not talk of her family background to anyone - least of all, Eleanor Capenhurst. Resting in Eleanor's hands was the reason. Siân Webster, nee Williams, had hated her up-bringing on the hill farm with such passion, that she had left home at sixteen years of age, determined under no circumstances to return. This was the first and only letter back to the family. It showed that what she had said during a heated argument before leaving for London remained as the truth; the close-knit family would not see her any more. The message was goodbye to her mother, father, grandparents and brother for ever.

How that letter, franked and delivered to the farm came to be among Siân's personal effects in southern England was a complete mystery. Only Siân and her Welsh family knew that six weeks after her emotional departure from Hendre Bach farm, Mr Williams had managed to draw a little money together. He travelled to London for the first time in his life and had arrived unannounced at the doctor's house in Belgravia Square, determined upon seeing his daughter and returning her horrid letter of rejection.

The sturdy, uncultivated figure of Owain Williams appeared at the servant's doorway and Siân had wanted to die. He was dressed up in his ancient shiny Sunday suit, a small, courageous fish well out of his own small pond, hill man's cap rolled tightly in a big gentle hand. Five minutes later, Owain was asked to leave and back in haughty Belgravia Square the harsh fact sunk in that his only daughter was, in all probability, lost to them for ever.

In truth, Eleanor didn't like Siân much. But she respected her intelligence and determination. The two women tolerated each other, had done for a long time, but last year they succumbed and fell to strong argument. Since Eleanor's move to this luxury apartment the two had not spoken a word. The worldly, English society hostess looked at her tea cup in shock. The letter was a bombshell. She finished her tea deep in thought and walked through to Jonathan's room. How would James react if she let the boy go to Wales? Would he blame her for not keeping his son safe as he had begged? She decided for Jonathan's sake it was the best and only thing she could do. She sat on the bed, ran fingers through his tangled hair as he sobbed, then moved to a little cushioned chair in the corner.

'If you really want to live with your Welsh grandparents, I could write to them. Would you like that?'

The boy sat up, rubbed his eyes and smiled. 'Will you, Aunt Eleanor, will you really?'

'Yes. And what is more, we could write it together. Come out with me now and I will ask Jeannette to bring ink, pen and paper. Will you help me?'

Jonathan beamed and jumped from the bed. They made their way out into the lounge to write the letter and make a new start together whilst Jonathan remained at Finsbury Park. It was true Eleanor had no idea at all if Jonathan's grandparents were alive, or Hendre Bach still existed near the little market town of Llanrwst, in far off Denbighshire. But at least she had an address on the envelope to work from.

Among the phases of a child's growth is a space where instinct can develop before maturity. Jonathan had begun to feel a strange confusion beneath his family pain. It frightened him. Silent memories were at last reaching out to draw the boy home because of this trauma and his ancient blood.

# Three

## Mountain Uplands Beneath Moel Seisiog, North Wales, Gt. Britain, June 1931.

Jonathan had been travel sick twice. The sickness had passed with the miles and what remained in the pit of his stomach was unyielding fear. The farmer's wife alone in her hot kitchen did not notice a whispering Rolls Royce motorcar as it turned off the narrow stony track outside and drew up quietly in the muddy yard unannounced.

Hendre Bach farm opened onto the cobble stoned yard by way of a five-bar gate. To the left, a farmhouse fashioned from rough hewn granite stone and capped with durable Caernarfon slate looked as Welsh and weathered as a Presbyterian miners' chapel. Half open sash windows drew fresh summer air through the rooms and white lime-washed walls soaked up pleasant warmth from the strengthening sunshine. Ahead of the black limousine, two buildings made up the far side of a quadrangle; a long stone barn to the left and, separated by a small path, a pig sty. Although the Rolls Royce had arrived in near silence, it drew grunts of disapproval from the pigs, bad tempered in their agitation, as the farmer's shire horse whinnied a cautious warning from his stable opposite the house.

The occupants of the stunning Silver Ghost motorcar sat for some seconds in their luxurious, cosseted surroundings; their uneasy mood increasing perceptibly with journey's end. The engine stopped. Its almost inaudible burble evaporated on a soft breeze and a few moments later the restless farm animals quit their mutterings.

The travellers had set out from London early the previous morning at an unhurried pace, staying overnight at Northampton Manor and apart from one or two minor delays were well ahead of schedule. Lady Denham-Hope's friend, the Honourable Eleanor Capenhurst sat in the rear with Jonathan who was looking outside at the farmyard in dismay. Both were travelling as distinguished guests of Her Ladyship. The Vicar of Capel Garmon had boarded their Rolls Royce from his rectory in Llanrwst and accompanied them to the farm on direct instructions from Archbishop Edwards, leader of The Church in Wales. Lady Denham-Hope had used her considerable influence once more.

Eleanor returned a quick, careful smile to the Welsh clergyman in the front passenger seat through the partition window. She looked every inch an aristocrat. Expensive clothes chosen to give the appearance of unassuming neutrality were somewhat misjudged for rural Wales; her lovely tailored cotton skirt, jacket, light summer coat and polished black boots gave a different impression to Huw Griffith's simpler, country-bred eyes. Jonathan looked lost beside her; Griffith could see it and felt the boy's pain.

'I'm afraid Mr Williams and his family will have been about their business since dawn.  A farmer's life is both arduous and time consuming, Mrs Capenhurst.  However, his wife is awaiting Jonathan's arrival as you requested.' The smile fell away from Reverend Griffith like a dropped curtain, a personal characteristic rather than a sign of disapproval and he indicated towards the house.  'Please listen.'

Eleanor lowered the car window and put her hand on Jonathan's, smiling at him to offer reassurance.  Together they peeped out across the farmyard. Hendre Bach was surrounded by a dramatic alpine beauty beyond a little dip in the green hillside on which the farmhouse was set. Jonathan had seen the peaks as the motorcar climbed and, at ten years of age, without one halfway decent memory of river or mountain to his name, felt lost beyond measure and wished for Croydon town with undisguised desperation. The kitchen door lay half open, no one could be seen, but Gwen Williams' clear, lilting voice carried out across the cobbled yard on heat-laden air.

The clergyman lifted his rather elderly bowler hat which had remained upon his head due to the high roof of the Rolls Royce, and placed it onto his lap with care.  'I am not one for singing, but being Welsh, I love the voice and its magnificent sounds...' They sat in silence; cocooned London elegance set before a proud rusticity which had seldom, if ever, come this close before.

Turning in his seat, Griffith looked at the boy with a twinkle in his eye and at the Englishwoman.  'This is a good and humble family, Mrs Capenhurst, the very best that our proud land can muster.  Your nephew will be well cared for here.' He indicated out of the window. 'She sings so beautifully.  There is no voice in all this world more lovely than a Welsh woman about her work. This young man will find no better home until his father may return to these shores!'

The remaining silence was stiff.  It was broken by Eleanor, asking Jonathan if he was ready to go in.  He made no reply, but looked at the lowered flap of a burr walnut drinks compartment built into the partition with the driver's cab.  On it stood a toy farm set.  The painted lead farm animals were laid out in a wide arc facing him; sheep, cows, pigs and horses, all placed in some absent minded game of escape.  Cat and mouse was at an end.  Jonathan continued staring at them.  Each creature seemed to be holding its breath, awaiting his sudden, irrevocable flood of tears.

'My brave little soldier...'

The Honourable Jonathan Ashbourne Webster was his father's son and he remained steadfast in resolve not to reveal one watery eye to anyone - in particular, his Aunt Eleanor.

She turned and hugged him, pulling him tight. 'Are you ready?'

The travellers looked to the farmhouse as sounds of domesticity and singing stopped. Jonathan stared with bated breath, watched the pitch black oak door swing open wide, and for the first time in his life laid eyes on his maternal grandmother. She was small, dressed in a long, simple dark dress with a white apron; her silvered auburn hair was tied back over a weathered brown face, features familiar to the boy - Welsh motherhood writ gentle and clear before him. Her bright, clever eyes were soft, but strong. They smiled and swung to the others.

'We weren't expecting...'

Across thirty feet the English lad read her joy in the startled expression.

'Please forgive me, Mrs Williams.' Eleanor's smile was immaculate. 'The journey took less time than I thought. If it is not convenient we can return later?'

'No, no, please...' Gwen Williams felt her emotions about to run away as her eyes returned to Siân's only son; tousle-haired bewilderment staring from the back seat of the majestic motorcar, a measure of wonder shining in his face which only a child can convey.

'If you would like to come through I will make some tea?'

Eleanor Capenhurst made to open the car door but the chauffeur did it for her. She walked across the muddy cobbles with care and took Gwen's small strong hand in hers. 'I am so pleased to meet you, Mrs Williams. It is so good of you to look after Jonathan...'

'Nonsense. The boy is my grandson.' No anger sparked in her sweet, lilting cadences, but it flashed for the briefest second in her eyes.

'Yes. But nonetheless...' Lord James Webster's sister lowered her voice, intimate and firm. 'I think it's best to make the break immediately. I'm sure you understand, Mrs Williams. The chauffeur can take my nephew's case through to his room and we will then leave. It is best that way - if we come into the house it may...'

Gwen held the titled woman's strong stare for a few moments and looked across to the boy. 'As you wish.'

Megan led Scraggs and Reverend Griffith through the house and up a narrow creaking staircase, each traveller carrying a heavy suitcase manfully whilst Jonathan stood outside the kitchen door. He managed to wipe away tears and raise a forced smile towards his aunt who had returned to the Rolls Royce. She was removing mud with painstaking care from her shiny boots using a small brush and cloth. A few minutes later the men returned and Scraggs coaxed the Rolls Royce back into whispering life. He turned it around with skill and heavy pulls on the large steering wheel, much head swivelling and hearty advice from the clergyman. After a brief, careful wave from an aunt to her nephew, they were gone.

Jonathan stood looking at the open farm gate, the falling lane outside; felt a warm breeze on his cheek, saw the steeply climbing green fields on the other side of the road. He turned slowly taking in as much as his tear threatening eyes would allow; stared at the white-washed farm buildings, heard the pigs grunting and saw the big brown head of Prince looking at him through the top of the opened stable door.

Gwen Williams kept herself in a corner of her kitchen until she felt her new grandson had the best chance of gathering his soaring emotions. Sensing her timing was right, she walked across the red-brown flagstones in near silence and stepped out into the yard.

Jonathan had his back to her. He was dressed in an expensive tweed jacket and short grey trousers, one sock had slipped to his ankle, a toy horse behind his back was clutched tightly in a small, clean white hand.

'Jonathan?'

The boy turned as if startled. His face lit up as he saw the Welsh lady up close. Bright hazel eyes like his mother's were shining at him, but in an older, lovely face. His other hand, inside the tweed jacket, was holding on to his father's solitary letter which had come from America a few days ago. It was destined to be read and re-read until tattered. He removed his hand and pocketed the toy horse. The Welsh lady bent down with care and they fell into each others arms. After a short period of cuddling, Gwen could feel his sobs inside her own.

'Come, cariad, this will never do. What will my other grandson say if he sees us blubbering like this?' She stood up holding him by the shoulders and turned to wipe a tear from her eye with the back of her hand. 'Have you got a hanky?'

He nodded. A shock of light brown hair on his forehead danced with the movement above freckled cheeks and he took out a folded and pressed handkerchief from the pocket of his trousers. They stood for a time regaining themselves and stepped inside; the kitchen was full of glorious cooking smells lifted on sumptuous heat from the simmering peat fired range. Jonathan stood still, staring after the Welsh lady as she walked along the huge flags and turned at the end by an open door. She promised to return in a few minutes and make him a cup of tea - he was to sit down and make himself at home.

The child looked around the actual room in which his mother had made her fateful decision to leave Wales and not return long before he was born. Jonathan took in the strange, ancient country things he saw about him with an easy mind. The Welsh oak dresser with willow pattern plates, pewter and clay mugs standing or hanging from hooks, a big black kettle steaming on a hook above the peat fire, a pot of meat and dumpling stewing on a griddle, lumpy lime-washed white stone walls, one tiny window, pieces of mutton and pork in muslin bags hanging from the rafters, the solemn tick of an ancient grandfather clock to his right, and the room's permanent, almost unbreakable silence. With some strange insight of heredity, the English boy could feel an instinctive love which the toil of generations had worked into these granite walls, strong oak beams and the smoothed flagstones beneath his feet, like the polishing of ancient leather. And this love was his as well. Jonathan was at a new, extraordinary beginning in his short life and saw his father with clarity as part of all the other things around him. He had no reaction other than surprise. The strong, distinctive face was smiling as only his father could. The English lad knew that he wasn't alone but didn't understand how he could see all this together in his head. The blood line of an ancient people, mingled with another of high birth had blended to open a rare door, which at ten years of age was like finding a new tooth in your mouth, or handstands are really easy to do.

*       *       *

And so I, as will-o'-the-wisp watched the boy's arrival; saw his father as Jonathan had seen him through mystical eyes, saw into his doughty soul. But was this scrap of humanity destined for the greatest of things under Her dominion? This and much else remained beyond my knowledge, yet I was learning fast.

I knew that within the boy's make up ran the Williams family's ancient Celtic line and also that of an English family, strong in Saxon heritage. The mix was special indeed. The doughty, unbroken connection from the Kings of old Saxony offered great strength. They were leaders of men and women who had arrived in England over a thousand years before, and this inherited genetic material from Saxon people would help to turn this boy into an extraordinary man one day; a

19

male whom She would use for the future good of humankind. More than this was beyond my ken.

I would be watching Jonathan's progress nonetheless and will meet with him soon when I inhabit Squire Bellamy's aristocratic body. The ticking of the clock had begun.

# Four

'Is he here yet, Mam?' William's Welsh words were gasped between lung fulls of air.

Megan beamed at her only son. 'Yes, they have arrived early. He is in the house with Nain.

'Hey! Going crazy, is it?' William's grandmother grabbed a fleeting arm as he rushed into the back kitchen, the boy was swung back, his own momentum lifting him from the floor. 'Now calm yourself this very minute and say hello to your cousin. Jonathan's come all the way from beyond London to stay with us until his father can return home.'

William stood up rubbing his arm and the boys looked at each other. Jonathan, his mouth full of oat cake, crumbs down his Fair Isle pullover beneath the tweed jacket stared in utter disbelief. Large brown eyes met those of the Welsh farm boy like a rabbit before a fox. William was dressed in a worn, black and grey waistcoat, holed shirt, shiny patched short trousers and worn leather boots tied up with string. The socks above the boots had holes in them. And the darkest eyes Jonathan had ever seen in his life were staring right back from under a mop of black curly hair.

'London, is it?'

'No.'

'Well, near is as good as.'

Jonathan nodded. They both paused, Gwen saying nothing, just watching like a proud mother hen.

'I can speak Cockney, see. We learnt at school.

'William!'

'It's true, Nain.' He grinned at his grandmother. 'Look lively, me old cocker, look lively!'

Jonathan nodded, chewing the last of his oat cake. 'That's right. That's cockney.' His freckled cheeks lifting into a grin then it was gone. 'Can't speak Welsh though. You have to in Wales or they do bad things to you; so I was told.'

'Like what?'

'Cut off your tongue with red hot scissors – Henry next door told me and he's been to Aberystwyth.'

William put his hands on his hips and laughed. He was tall and lanky for a twelve-year-old. The shock of black curls crowned a strong, broad young face with expressive Celtic features that could be read like a picture book. 'You're talking rubbish, man.' He looked at his Nain and back at the English boy. 'We might throw you in the river, that's all.'

Gwen admonished him once more, but Jonathan could see a faint smile about her lips and a twinkle in those lovely, distinctive eyes like his mother's.

'Finished your tea, Jonathan?'

He nodded, slurped the rest and wiped his mouth on his handkerchief.

'Then William will show you round the farm, won't you William?'

Jonathan watched his new companion give a half-hearted shrug, put strong brown hands into his short trouser pockets, making fists of them and push hard to the bottom. The English boy could see a rip in the left pocket and the obvious threadbare condition of the farm boy's clothes made him feel conspicuous.

'Can you run? I'll not dawdle about.'

'Course I can run.'

'Fast?'

'Fast enough.'

'For what?'

'Depends.'

'Can you climb trees?'

'What?'

William's dark eyes looked as if they were about to pop. 'You'd best learn fast. I'm the best climber between here and Betws-y-Coed.'

Gwen turned from the cooking range where she was inspecting the mutton stew through a cloud of steam. 'Go on with you, braggart. Get outside and show Jonathan around. You've got hours to go before supper but I want you back for chores well beforehand.' She stared at the two lads sternly, but those eyes twinkled with love. 'Go on, the pair of you, and be quick about it.' As the kitchen door closed behind them, Mrs Williams looked after, a happy smile coursing her weathered face. He looked such a sweet boy, so gentle and self-effacing, and so uncommonly good looking, with lovely brown hair and dark fluid eyes like an animal's - another six or seven years would see the girls queuing. She put down a kitchen knife and opened the door. 'When you've shown Jonathan the yard and the animals, take him up to see Nain and Taid Hafod. If they're out, you could walk down to the river together - but no tomfoolery, mind.'

'Yes, Nain.' William looked at the newcomer, 'Look lively then,' they turned on their heels together and shot out across the cobblestone quadrangle where the Rolls Royce had been standing half an hour before. Prince was looking out of the stable door, whites of his eyes showing and twitching his ears with apparent expectation as the boys walked across. The horse snorted, surveyed them cautiously and whinnied.

'Go on, Jon. Pat his head. He'll not hurt you.' The Welsh lad demonstrated with a strong, gentle brown hand and grinned. Jonathan put out a careful arm but withdrew it fast, his freckle-face solemn.

William's gangly frame stiffened, wiry arms were hooked onto his slim hips. 'Oh dear...frightened, is it? Look lively then!' He shot off at speed down the cobbled yard with his English protégé hard on his heels. They turned by the end of the stable, sprinted along a narrow track under the dark branches of a broad oak tree giving cool flecks of shady colour to the hard earth path and finished up at a stone hay barn with a corrugated, rusty-red tin roof. William knelt down and pulled a large handful of hay from a bale and re-routed back to Prince's stable through a vegetable garden; his nimble feet skipping around plants, canes and obstacles at testing speed with arms lifted in a sort of balancing act to impress. They arrived back in less than a minute and William looked hard at his English cousin.

'You're gasping.'

'No I'm not.'

'Looks like it to me.'

'Well I'm not.'

'You need to make friends, see.' He indicated to the huge shire. 'Give him this hay.'

Jonathan was scared but did as he was bid, doing his best to hide the fear.

'Now pat him.'

The hair on the big horse's face and neck felt soft and warm to the English lad's soft hands.

'See. He likes you. You've just made friends! C'mon.'

They shot off, rattling across the cobbles to the pig sty.

'You ever seen real pigs close to?' William's dark Celtic features were inquisitive.

The shorter boy looked over the stone wall to a food trough. He wrinkled his nose.

'You're a townee.' William jumped up and sat on top of the wall, his knees dirty from the hay barn. 'Is Croydon a town?'

'Of course it's a town - but we have pigs, horses and stuff too.'

'In a town?'

'No. Nearby.'

'You don't like pigs, do you?'

'No.'

They looked at Cadi. She was fat, snuffling, with six piglets about her.

'She's a good saddleback. Pigs is cleaner than dogs!' William nodded hard. 'It's true. And they're intelligent.'

'Why do they wallow around in sties then?'

"Cos man puts them there, that's why. Pigs keep their bedding straw clean as you keep a bed!'

Jonathan looked into the sty, said nothing and wrinkled his nose once more to show he meant it.

'Taid says you can eat everything but the squeak...' He looked unemotionally at the animals. 'Cadi will be killed this autumn - she'll feed us all for months and months.' He picked a piece of cabbage out of the hole and threw it in the trough. 'Come on then, we haven't got all day.'

They ran down a narrow passage between the sty and the end of a whitewashed stone barn, counted thirteen hens and one cockerel in the chicken run, dashed out across the springy sheep-cropped turf of Cae Bach. William was rather surprised with the younger boy's agility. He guessed Jonathan to be a good year younger than him - maybe two. With ever increasing desperation, William cavorted around. The English lad's expensive tweed jacket swung from side to side as he ran after in excited zig-zags, shouting good-hearted replies to the challenges. Whatever the Welsh farmer's son did, he couldn't lose him. They worked their way along the L-shape of Cae Bach and around the back of the farmhouse to a five-bar-gate which fronted a narrow stony road.

'Who's panting now?'

'You are, Jon.'

'Never...'

They climbed the gate and dropped down running onto the road together. Opposite lay the rising slope of hendre pastures with the more mountainous hafod lifting away in steep, scattered grassland beyond. The boys ran across the road shouting. Nature was bursting with her wonderful fertility all about them - sweet green grass, a few flowers un-cropped by sheep and warming in the bright sunshine. About sixty yards from the road a small stream glinted diamond light, wending its way down the hendre to a coppice resplendent with early summer flowers. All over the sunlit pasture, Mr Williams's sheep were grazing contentedly. Higher up, a few stunted trees remained on the more abrupt slopes. Heather, yellow flowered gorse and broom together with stands of bracken increased their presence as the long incline lifted a rugged way up to the hafod. The remainder was hidden beyond the sweep of the hills set beautifully against a bright blue sky. Jonathan's sharp eyes took in the scene as they crossed the little stony road and he turned to William.

'Who are we going to see?'

'Nain and Taid Hafod.' William pointed over the high slope. 'They live up there.' He slowed and stopped for a few seconds. 'They're your family too, Jon.'

'Mine?' Jonathan stared into the broad features, trying to take William's ragged appearance in and dirty face from their exertions in the vegetable garden; the Welsh boy's eyes were clear, his face shining through the smudges.

'Aye. They're your great grandfather and great grandmother as well as mine. They're very old.' He pushed back his shock of black curls. 'We say Nain Hafod and Taid Hafod because they live there and it's easier. In Wales, with so many Jones's and Evans's and the like, a man takes on the name of his farm or his job - it's tradition, see.'

'Dai the Milk?'

'Aye.'

'Is the lady who went up to get you when we arrived your mum?'

'Aye.'

'Where's your dad?'

'Are all townees like you?'

Jonathan shrugged his shoulders, eyes fixed hard on his amazing Welsh cousin and they broke into a trot across the springy turf.

'He was a hero; killed nearly fifty Germans before they got him.'

'A soldier?'

'Aye.'

'In the Great War?'

'Aye.'

William changed the trot to a run with intent.

'Got any more questions, lad?'

The newcomer shook his head and just before reaching a bubbling stream they turned up the hafod at a faster pace. From nowhere, a great hare shot out of a gully near their feet; it skirted around them and bounded away down the rich meadowlands. The boys stopped, watching the creature leap away in seconds.

'That's Tomos. He has his lair up on the hafod somewhere. This place is a paradise for a big hare like him. He likes to bask out in the sun. There is a long dingle ahead carved out by this lively old stream, plenty of heather and sweet mountain grasses, many a covering of gorse or broom where he can make cosy dens and many sheep walks for him to play along. Hare is a rare old delicacy, Jon, but neither Taid, nor Taid Hafod have been able to shoot old Tomos - he's just too cunning for them.'

Soon the boys were running alongside the gurgling torrent, following it by way of a winding sheep track. They climbed upward, around stony outcrops and on through scattered bushes of prickly gorse towards the upland pastures.

The small amount of puppy fat on Jonathan was deceptive, he was muscular and strong for his age, yet the steep incline and William's hard pace had him almost beaten by the time they stopped to cross a tiny road. The soft, town-bred cousin William had been expecting was proving to be a real surprise - a friend in the making perhaps and someone who just might show the best climber this side of Betws-y-Coed, a clean pair of heels one day.

They looked back. Not a house, or a living soul could be seen from their high aerie. Foothills each side of the River Conwy rose steeply and the life which sheltered at the valley's floor was completely hidden. On the other side of the valley, Mount Snowdon and her sisters stood out in cold, isolated splendour - crystal clear sunlight brightening sombre grey flanks, deep ridges and shale slopes where dwarves and trolls might live; like a fairy tale made real. William was panting, but he grinned at his companion. 'Look lively, me old cocker. Look lively!'

The two set off up the last of the slope at a faster pace, Jonathan more determined than ever not to be beaten in spite of a chest which was threatening to burst apart before he could go much further.

'Crown land this. But Taid has grazing rights for all his sheep,' he swept an arm around, 'to the wall up there. Look. Nain and Taid Hafod's cottage!'

Jonathan blinked ahead at a ragged white cliff. Strange turrets of rock guarded the brink, and beneath them, tucked away in a ragged corner, as if in the crook of a stony old elbow, stood a long single storey cottage built out of rough, moss covered boulders with an uneven grey slate roof. The English refugee blinked his wet eyes for a while. He did not want William to see a weakling's tears and pointed. 'There?'

'Aye. C'mon.' William leapt a gully like a fox and sped over towards the rocky plateaux.

They ran forward, William jumping boulders and leaping rain gullies to provoke, arms held high, and Jonathan obliging him by copying every move until they reached Hafod cottage's blue-grey boundary made from large slabs of slate. These looked like a hundred grave stones set in a large rectangle around the cottage. Within this enclosure, the thin mountain earth, clinging onto rocky bones of the high land, had been worked over many years and turned into a splendid kitchen garden full of the most gorgeous vegetables and herbs. They ran down a path of beaten earth and stones to an ancient black oak door; upon it the date of 1694 had been carved in unrefined letters to stand out in relief above an old iron latch. Jonathan had never seen a house anything like Hafod in his life before and looked at the dwelling wide-eyed. A house of witches he thought. The thick bouldered walls were mortared with a mixture of clay and lime, small diamond-paned windows set deep into the lichen-patterned exterior glinted from the bright sun overhead.

William knocked on the door, it was unlocked, and he lifted the iron latch and pushed the door open.

'Taid, Nain - you there? It's William and a friend.' The words were in Welsh. He turned to Jonathan. 'No one in.'

A wonderful smell of cooking greeted them as they stepped inside. Cottage furniture, a table, stools and a large cupboard appeared out of the dim light. Scattered on the floor were a profusion of rush mats and at the far end of the long, oak-beamed room stood an old cast iron stove, its cheery little doors wide open from recent attention. On top, a big black pan was simmering gently. William lit a taper from the peat fire inside the stove and fixed it into a chink in the wall. Both lads were hot from the climb and they quenched their thirsts with icy cool rainwater from a stone jug in the pantry. William turned his attention to the big pan. He found a wooden spoon and dipped it in.

'Come and taste this, Jon. Cawl nain - granny's broth! Bet you've never tasted its like before.'

Jonathan hadn't. A portion of sheep, boiled to a wonderful softness with potatoes, vegetables and flavoured with many herbs had been left to simmer all day, allowing complimentary flavours to be mixed and brought through to perfection.

William waited until his new cousin had finished a spoonful or two, he spoke loudly. 'Nain Hafod's a witch!'

The English boy jumped. He could see William's face in the taper-light, the boy's eyes were sparkling. 'When I first saw this cottage I thought...'

'No, no. Not a real witch, lad. But you English might think so.'

'Why?'

'Nainy's our doctor. She doctors most people on the farms this side of Llanrwst.'

'A witch doctor?'

The dark features frowned and William pulled the taper out from the wall. 'Perhaps. C'mon, I'll show you.' He lifted the latch of a door next to the stove. It opened onto a narrow whitewashed passage with a door off to one side and another at the far end. They walked through and entered a low room. It was of surprising size and filled almost to overflowing with long wooden benches, cupboards and shelves. These in turn bore many stone jars, pots, plates, wicker baskets and were filled with every plant, weed, flower and herb one could think of. Under the tiny single diamond-paned window was a slate shelf with a pestle and mortar upon it. Next to the shelf stood a little oaken table with a large brass-bound black book.

'Nain Hafod's medicine room!' William indicated to the array. 'I've collected a lot of the plants here for her. Nain used to take me out when I was four or five, showing me things she wanted and how to find them. We'd walk fifteen miles in a day if we walked one.'

'What are they for?'

'Everything to make you strong. Nain Hafod can make someone better if they're ill, stronger if they're weak. Her potions cheer a body up when they're down, or cool the nerves if they've been frazzled. She can cure most things in man or beast - broken limbs or a broken heart!' He winked. 'Now she's your Nain Hafod too! Look -'

He took the English boy over to the black book lying on the little table and undid a metal clasp on its faded cover. A worn old waistcoat over a holed shirt, shiny patched short trousers and twelve child-summers in rural Denbighshire seemed an unconvincing connection with book-learning, but the farm boy knew his way into the gold-edged pages as if a regular scholar. William eased the old leaves open with great care and pointed to the title page which read:

OLDE RECIPES, REMEDIES & NATURE-LORE
by Doctor Elias Williams

At the bottom of the page was the name of a printer in Chester and the date, 1760.

'Nain Hafod says Taid's great, great, great grandfather had this book printed. He was a clever medical doctor who studied nature's plants for remedies and they worked!' He looked at Jonathan and turned to the back of the big book. 'At the end used to be a lot of blank pages, but Nainy Hafod has filled almost every one with her own prescriptions for things.'

To Jonathan, this seemed pretty close to witchcraft. He wasn't exactly scared. The Welsh boy, son of his mother's brother was the closest young relative he had and although the two boys had barely formed a friendship, Jonathan liked William, he even trusted him now. The strange feeling about witches was more to do with finding out one of his own ancestors had been something akin to a wizard hundreds of years ago, and now he had a great grandmother who still dabbled - a sort of Welsh, Old Mother Shipton. Jonathan had gleaned scary facts about this venerable Yorkshire character from Mrs Eldridge, his mother's housekeeper, as they had sat by the fireside in Croydon on rainy days and winter evenings. Now he was grateful for her tales of unusual things.

'See the drawings, Jon - wonderful work...'

Jonathan peeped over the farm boy's shoulder and gaped at the old pages marked with age and use. What once must have been fine penmanship of some unknown draughtsman - copying Doctor Williams's original drawings, perhaps - stepped off the ancient leaves from over 170 years, thrilling the cousins immensely. Hundreds of hand-made drawings filled the great book, their colours remaining bright, although the ink lines were brown and faded after all this time; but to the boys they were looking at a world of magic. Beside each picture was a description made in an old-fashioned illuminated print, including medical properties the good doctor claimed for each plant. He gave the readers significant information for the recognition of herbage, collection and how to effect real cures to innumerable ailments - many quite serious. All who wished to avail themselves of nature's benevolence only had to follow Doctor Williams's explicit instructions, so claimed the short preface.

As Jonathan was reading these opening words, William disappeared among the wooden shelves and returned with a recent addition, which he laid on the small table next to the book. He waited patiently for Jonathan to finish reading and took over, turning through the pages with care, his deft brown fingers showing he knew what he was about. William stopped and pointed. 'There. St John's Wort. The drawing's a good likeness, isn't it?'

Jonathan peered and nodded. 'Does it do anything?'

'Do anything?' William laughed good-naturedly. 'Course it does. These big green leaves help to heal wounds - they stop pain too.' He pulled his shirt sleeve and indicated to a clean, well healed scar on his forearm. 'Nain Hafod put some leaves on this when I cut it with a knife, a year back now. Pain went after five minutes. It got better in days. Do you believe me?'

Jonathan nodded.

William dropped down on his haunches, stared up and winked. 'I can show you something down in Squire's Wood that's much, much better than anything here in Nain Hafod's medicine room. That's if you trust me?' He waited for a response but got none.

'Interested?'

Jonathan's eyes flashed around the room nervously and rested on his new friend. 'If Nain Hafod returns and catches us here will we be in trouble?'

'Aye.'

'We ought to go then?'

'Aye. We ought to go.' William stood up and closed the book with care. 'Scared, are you?'

'Of what?'

'Witches an' things.'

The English lad shrugged. 'This is my first day. I don't want to get into trouble on my first day.'

'No.'

'Shall we go?'

'Aye. We'll go. Nain Hafod won't mind us being here. I can come and go any time I like with the plants. She's used to it.'

'And me?'

'Maybe you're right - till she gets to know you, eh?'

The two paused, looking around the room.

'What about your secret, then?'

'Secret?'

'Yes. In Squire's Wood.'

William flushed a little. 'Well, I don't really know if I can trust you, do I?'

'Trust me?'

'Aye. That's right. Trust you...' William rung his clever hands. 'Squire's a funny cove - mad some say; stark raving mad say others...'

The darkest eyes Jonathan had ever seen in his life were staring out knowingly from his new friend's wily face. 'Come on then. That is, if you really want to find out about our mad Squire.'

## Five

## Three and a Half Weeks Later

A bright and breezy Sunday morning saw the Williams family up early as usual, except for Jonathan who remained in bed. William was sent upstairs and gleefully pulled him out at 7.15 a.m. Farm work had been dauntingly hard, seemingly all consuming, and the little free time left had not allowed them to visit Squire's Wood, but that would come soon enough.

The English stripling had endured a significant culture upset from his suburban life in southern England. Considering the huge change, he was fitting in well enough. So far, Mrs Williams had allowed him to miss Church each Sunday morn, initially because he had understandably been tired from the changes to his life. But this third Sunday was different. Her new grandson was going to Church with the rest of the family and that was that.

In their spare time, William and Jonathan were inseparable. Time off was generous considering the heavy work load farm life demanded from everyone, but in terms of Jonathan's middle-class world of English private day school and the many friends with whom he played in the richer parts of Surrey's stockbroker belt, it was tiny - and his resentment was growing fast. William, in the next bed, got up with the cockcrow around 5.30 every day, including Sundays and without any complaint. The tiny upstairs bedroom they shared had been Jonathan's mothers long ago. Gwen Williams had told him so and although happy there, it imparted an odd feeling nonetheless, as if something beyond his ken was beginning to happen which he did not yet understand and was wholly powerless to resist.

In less than a month, blisters developed, then harder skin and a corporeal knowledge of Mr Williams's kitchen crops together with experience of many trying tasks on the sheep dotted forty-five acres. Potatoes, peas, carrots, swedes and runner beans grew in seemingly endless rows across the dark, rich soil between Prince's stable and the chicken run, but these were no longer things just found in greengrocers shops. Nothing which his now hardening hands lifted, weeded between or inspected were cultivated there purely for pleasure, for friends to savour, or lovingly molly-coddled for the local show. Each plant had its own part to play in the real physical act of survival for the Welsh family. Income as hard cash was rare, so everything that could be grown, made or reared was produced and greatly valued at Hendre Bach. The ten-year-old blue-blood had felt the strong bite of its harsh labour, for he was now a farmer's boy and school holidays had many weeks yet to run.

Peat, fuel for cooking and winter heating, they cut high up on hafod land at Fawnog-fawr. Black, wet peat, sliced into rectangular blocks by Mr Williams with his special spade made for the purpose, whilst he sang out happily among the breezes in his lovely baritone voice. Each piece was then laid out by the boys for drying in the warm July winds - plentiful up there now, among misty mountains beyond the distant Conwy river in a picture book panorama. They returned when the blocks were dried, at least as far as the weather had allowed, Prince pulling the big wooden wain down to the hendre, it stacked high with partly dry peat blocks looking like solidified treacle and Jonathan as tired as a virgin navvy holding the reins manfully, the farmer, his pipe burning strongly, giving out gentle instructions to two loved grandsons among curling wreaths of cheerful blue smoke.

When back, they rolled in behind the big shire and across to the long stone barn at the edge of the yard; then the hard work returned as they carried blocks of peat inside. The Williamses had a good area set aside where it could be fully dried out, becoming brown and dusty and ready as excellent fuel. Nain baked her beautiful bread in the same long stone barn, buying her yeast and freshly milled wheat flour from a shop in Llanrwst, about six miles away. Her oven was near the end of the barn and Jonathan found a simple pleasure in watching her move the freshly baked loaves in and out with a long metal spade. The warmth and smell of it all made a wonderful panacea to blisters and aching bones.

Nain, or Megan, William's mam, would also wash clothes there in a dolly-tub, using a wooden rod with a handle and three prongs sticking out at the other end to work the clothes. The family called the dolly rod, dobio - thumper - because Megan used to hit William with it if he was very naughty.

The animals were all fed routinely and their quarters cleaned out. Pero and Moss, no relation to Owain Williams's original sheep dogs from way back when Siân was a girl, for they had long since died, were keen to work. Work to a hardy mountain sheep dog seemed to be no work at all, but life as it should be lived; a restless instinctive and simple creature viewing the world from his perspective fifteen inches above the ground - four itchy feet included. To run twenty miles a day across open hills of sheep-cropped turf, about boulders and scree slopes in almost any weather was not labour at all for Pero and Moss, but merely life.

The boys were out on the hillside with their grandfather in all weathers, moving the flock to newer grasses, helping with yearlings, watching out for predators under ragged windswept skies. And twice now, since Jonathan had been there, Mr Williams had taken the boys shooting rabbits around the kitchen garden after plants had been damaged. That was the very best job of all! Jonathan was much taken by the farmer's ornately engraved double barrelled shotgun. It used to belong to Taid Hafod, Mr Williams's father-in-law who lived with his wife up at Hafod cottage where the boys had been on that first day, peeking a look at the great book of herbal remedies held in Nain Hafod's medicine room.

So, at Hendre Bach farmhouse lived Jonathan and William's Nain and Taid and William's mother, Megan. Up at Hafod Cottage lived Nain and Taid Hafod, William and Jonathan's great grandparents. Compared with the softer lifestyle of the English boy's suburban Croydon home, this harsh but happy environment had fashioned a naturally closely knit, powerful family unit, which unknown to him, was just beginning to ease bitter wounds in his young heart.

Gwen Williams pumped hard on the leather bellows before her kitchen fire grate that Sunday morning, embers glowed red, then burst into bright life under Jack Moog the blackened copper hood. Smoke and ash disappeared into the stone chimney breast as she added more blocks of peat to the fire, then turned to work at the range. The rest of the Williams family, except for Megan who was helping with chores, were sitting around the long deal kitchen table dressed in their Sunday best clothes. They were awaiting Sunday breakfast and Church with similar expectations, each to satisfy different hungers in different ways. Jonathan opened the kitchen door and walked in, his chubby, freckle-face sullen and dejected. He was dressed in his expensive tweed jacket, Fair Isle pullover and best short grey trousers as Nain had instructed, all ready for Church. The dark eyes of his father flashed as they all greeted him in cheerful chorus.

'Duw, you look smart, Jonathan, make your mam proud.' Owain Williams's large white teeth flashed in a smile out of his weathered, kindly face. 'Come on, sit up beside me for your breakfast.'

He indicated as Megan turned, blue eyes sparkling, a happy smile lifting her pretty face. 'Come on, Jonathan. Sit here opposite William or you'll be too late!' She pushed her corn coloured hair away gently with slim, long-fingered hands and joined Gwen by the cooking range, the grace of a young mother about her.

Jon Bach sat down and William grinned mischievously, pleased that it wasn't him on the receiving end this time. He pursed his lips and wide eyes watched the older boy as he whispered quickly across the table. 'If you don't eat your breakfast Taid will cut out your tongue with red hot scissors!'

'Be quiet, William.'

'Then you'll be sent to Aberystwyth.'

William ducked suddenly as Taid swung a half serious hand across the back of his grandson's head.

'Enough of that. Now eat up!'

And so they did. Megan brought a plate of eggs and Gwen a plate of bacon. They all tucked in to a wonderful breakfast of home produced ham, eggs and Nain's lovely home cooked bread which tasted as good as it smelt, hot and crispy straight out of the oven, with butter made by Nain Hafod in her cottage, even though she was nearly eighty years of age. Megan made splits in each hunk of bread so that the butter melted through inside. The Sunday breakfast was washed down with lashings of hot tea and by the end, even sulky Jonathan had cheered up a little.

As the women washed up, Taid and the two boys cleaned their boots under the window with Pero and Moss sniffing inquisitively.

The family left the kitchen at 8 a.m. to the guarding presence of their two collies, and the solemn grandfather clock in the corner. The first service in English was two hours away at ten. This left enough time to meet Nain and Taid Hafod as they came down the rich meadows opposite Hendre Bach, then the whole family would walk the three miles down Pen y Rhiwlas to Capel Garmon under the brooding company of the Snowdon Horseshoe on the other side of the valley. Jonathan and William's great grandfather and great grandmother were exceptional at being able to walk such a distance still – but around the Conwy Valley Celtic people of such advanced years could still be seen travelling long distances on foot that would put younger people in towns to shame. The summer weather usually allowed everyone to wear their Church-going shoes. When the weather was poor, they carried them in raffia bags or wrapped them up in parcels and wore rubber boots. Mud spatterings in the winter time appeared over best clothes soon after they left the farm, Taid told Jon Bach that it just couldn't be helped. No one minded because most of the congregation had similar problems. Snow made it worse of all, but they usually got through.

As the family walked up the stony road and over the hill outside the farmhouse, Nain and Taid Hafod appeared crossing the meadow within a few minutes. Elias Jones, farmer, eighty-two years of age and sprightly still, was dressed in best social wear as was Morfydd, his wife. Their weathered faces brightened immediately they saw Jonathan in new clothes he had brought from England, his image veritably shining to their old eyes - so Gwen had put her foot down after all and the boy was going to Church. Good! They were so proud. Such a lovely, good looking young fellow, reminding Morfydd so much of her granddaughter, Siân, who had been away from them all these fourteen years past. Nain Hafod lifted the hem of a long grey dress over the stones at the side of the road, her wrinkled, black boots shining. She smiled her cheery, red-cheeked smile and Taid Hafod lifted his bowler hat in greeting.

'Get that gun o' mine out soon as you like, Owain. Seen more rabbits up on Hafod than ever!'

The hat, dark serge suit and silk waistcoat had seen over thirty years of use at least, but restricted to weddings, funerals and Sunday worship had kept things looking fairly respectable, nonetheless.

The two men fell to conversation and soon the family were turning down from the Nebo road towards the long, steep incline of Rhiwlas. Owain liked his father-in-law. In spite of being well over eighty, the elderly man's mind was bright and the two liked talking over their pipes and glasses of ale with friends down in the village when time could be found, which was rare enough now. The day was a pleasant one. Not too warm for walking and not too cold if one stopped for the odd early blackberry or to stare at the world. Gwen called William to her side and gave him a quiet talking to, for he was inclined to wander ahead and jump out at them from behind rocks or out from a group of ash trees further down Rhiwlas, just for sheer devilment. And their new charge, Jonathan was unquestionably in a mood anyway after being dragged from his Sunday morning bed - she didn't want the pair getting up to mischief together. A warm wind had freshened on the higher ground, but as the family walked on among the cover of folding green hill slopes, it eased away to a gentle stillness. Megan was the quietest of them all and walked beside her mother-in-law contently, giving the odd curt word to William as she felt sure that he was up to something in his head. For the first time the boys were not playing or clowning together, yet she was so pleased that William had a real friend now. As they traipsed through flower-decked meadow-lands, Jonathan Webster fell ever further behind and they decided to let things be and see if he perked up, a quiet consensus was then agreed upon and everyone fell to happier talk.

Jonathan watched his surrogate family moving slowly away, but didn't care at all. He kicked at a dead branch sticking out from under a hawthorn bush and looked up at the white matrix of cloud high above. It was streaked by many fingered channels cutting across the bright blue as billow raced billow towards the distant horizon. He felt really bleak and wished with everything in him to be anywhere but Wales right now. Then the truth dawned. Up until now, he hadn't been given a chance to feel bleak about anything because of all the back-breaking work Mr Williams, in particular, had allotted to him. The English boy wondered about his mother, then his father in America and looked at hardy Welsh relatives stepping nimbly along the faint track which vanished and reappeared capriciously across meadow and dell, taking them further and further from his sight down an increasingly steep hillside. A distinctive vista had appeared, like one of the lovely coloured pictures he had at home in an illustrated encyclopedia, but this picture had Capel Garmon village at its heart and it seemed to be an unbearably long way off. The aristocrat's son felt utterly depressed at the thought of some bumbling old vicar and then an even more dismal walk home.

'Where's Jon Bach?' Mrs Williams turned from a conversation with Nain Hafod, her lovely hazel eyes suddenly brightly fierce. 'Where's the boy got to? William, why haven't you kept your eye on him?'

'You never said I've got to keep my eye on him!'

'Shush.' She turned back up the hill as her newly acquired grandson came into view around a craggy rock covered in pieces of moss and lichen. His hands were in his pockets and he was looking down in an absentminded way, kicking at the dead branch forlornly.

Mrs Williams stalked up the hill slope, silent and angry, strands of her silvery grey hair flying in the wind until she was within ear-shot.'

'Jonathan!'

His head jerked up instantly.

'You'll make us all late if you don't get a move on.'

'I'm tired, Grandmother.'

Gwen stopped before him, still breathing easily in spite of the incline. 'No, Jonathan. I'm called Nain.' Her lilting Welsh cadences cut through the breeze like a knife. He knew she was angry but didn't care.

'Nain. And I've worked ever so hard all week and now you want me to walk all the way to Church.'

'Is it a soft grandson I've got here then?' Gwen put her hands on her hips and glared, more for effect than actual anger, for in an instant it had eased to a simmer. 'Do you not go to Church in Croydon?'

Jonathan rallied. 'No I don't. I don't like them. But I could if I wanted to. Churches aren't miles and miles away from anywhere like here.'

'Jonathan!'

'It's silly walking miles over mountains and stuff...' The boy hung his head.

'It might be miles to walk, but walking will do a growing young man like you some good.'

The dark eyes of Lord Webster flashed angrily for a moment in his son as the freckled face lifted. 'I don't want doing good. I'm tired. William said there are wild animals up here and they can attack people!'

'So why are you dawdling then?'

Gwen felt her husband's strong, gentle hand on her shoulder, but the Welshman's smile was for his new grandson alone.

'This is a long trek down for a boy more used to trains, buses and I dare say motorcars, now.' He winked, the big leather face creasing like a cushion under his brown countryman's cap. 'You like a ride on my shoulders, Jon Bach?' Owain was a tough survivor, but wise enough to feel sorry for a boy who had both his parents desert him - whatever the rights and wrongs of their departure - and if the youngster's emotions had stumbled a little now, a touch of kindness probably would not go amiss. Jonathan's eyes flicked defensively towards his grandmother and back in a second. 'Yes sir.'

'No sirs up here, boy.'

'Taid.'

'Taid.' The canny Welsh hill farmer nodded and bent his back, allowing the ten-year-old to climb carefully onto his broad shoulders; then he ambled off, gait unchanged, his pace the same constant easy rhythm he used when climbing a hillside or crossing his own farmyard. Whoops of joy were now coming from Jonathan as William and Megan arrived, they were followed by Nain and Taid Hafod who were puffing, but wouldn't have been pleased by its mention.

'Jon Bach's a little tired so he's getting a ride.'

'Can I have a ride too, Taid?'

Everyone gathered around the farmer.

'What both of you together?'

'Oh, yes please.'

Mr Williams laughed out aloud, a big, hearty laugh like an echo in a cwm. 'I'm not Atlas holding the world up, boy!'

Gwen took his arm as the party moved off again. She smiled. 'You at choir practice this evening, Owain?'

'No.  Not 'til next week.'

They turned down a path with ancient dry stone walls each side which were dressed generously in round leaved pennywort, tight, squat groups of house leeks looking like rose flowers and green clumps of saxifrage mixed among an extravagant display of multi-coloured lichen in browns, reds, speckled greys, greens and yellows for those with eyes to see.  At the foot of the walls, honeysuckle, wild garlic and foxgloves grew in profusion.  The rutted path led to Glyn Pig's farmyard, so named for his manners rather than his Pen y livestock, but they turned off a hundred yards or so before the gate.  In the silence, wing-beats of crows could be heard as they flew high above and the hum of insects was everywhere.  Ten minutes saw any remaining vestiges of human habitation left behind as the last part of Rhiwlas swallowed the party.  Soon, old Taid Hafod, without any prompting started singing a hymn in practice for Church and Morfydd joined him with her gentle contralto voice.

*'Guide me, O thou great Redeemer,*
*Pilgrim through this barren land;*

Gwen and Megan joined in the first of the three famous choruses, lifting it on wings:

*Bread of heaven,*
*Bread of heaven,*
*Feed me now and evermore,*

Owain's, smooth baritone voice blended with Taid Hafod's tenor, repeating the last word in harmony and then the whole family sang the last line *rallentando* with an ease as if they had been following a Church choir.

Jonathan looked down in quiet astonishment from Owain's shoulders.  His twelve-year-old cousin had joined the adults spontaneity as if turning hay in the sun or running the flock into cae bach.  Nothing like music lessons at school in Croydon - nothing forced or contrived - as if it were the most natural thing in the world to sing.  The voices lifted again.

*'Open now the crystal fountain*
*Whence the healing stream doth flow;*
*Let the fiery cloudy pillar*
*Lead me all my journey through.'*

The Williamses strolled on happily, across fields and past outcrops of rock fronting conifer trees with rooks searching around their pinnacles for a resting place, the great Welsh hymn drifting across the open, breath taking vista of the Conwy Valley.

When the last chorus came to a rousing end, Owain called up through the contrasting empty, but happy chatter which remained. 'Jonathan, why don't you like going to Church?'

The farmer had climbed over a stile at the top of Ianto's highest field among the family's lilting start at Myfanwy before a reply came; his now cheerful, chuckling load still in place whilst friendly taunts and grimaces were being tossed between the two boys.

'Church is boring.' Jonathan stared at Nain holding Taid's arm beneath him. 'And I don't like singing... I don't think there's a God anyway!'

Gwen smiled up at her new grandson, which he wasn't expecting, then Taid bent down as the boy was starting to fidget and let him climb off.

William couldn't help over hearing and he was fascinated. Fancy having a cousin who didn't believe in God and said so too! He wondered if Jonathan would tell the vicar - he was in a mad enough mood to do so, too - wow! Perhaps the vicar would throw him out? The Welsh lad was wild at the thought, he didn't mind Church, he had never known anything else really, Auntie Rhian's teas beforehand were nice and he liked the chance of using his pea-shooter at the people outside from a really good hiding place hidden behind the short yew trees either side of the Church door. This had been going on for months - on and off - and Taid now suspected him strongly, in spite of denials. Serious threats of dobio being used again made it even more exciting, adding an edge so that he was even quicker getting out of the way after a good shot! Jonathan had made a good pea-shooter as well. Just suppose his cousin told the vicar that he didn't believe in God...

Grandfather and new grandson ambled off through Ianto's bleating flock of ewes, leading the seven towards the farmhouse, still out of sight about 500 yards distance. The unrefined Welshman took his pipe out, filled it and soon cheerful blue smoke was rising again. He looked down at Jonathan kindly. 'You've learned a bit since coming to us, eh, Jon Bach?'

The boy's eyes lifted for a moment. 'Yes, Taid!'

The pipe had a nice masculine, grandfather smell. Even with the breeze lifting across the ffridd Jonathan could now recognise Owain's pipe tobacco easily.

'When I was your age, young Jon Bach, my great grandfather, hen daid as we say in the Welsh, was alive. Now he was a glorious old man, a real countryman. He first taught me to notice the muted colours on the land, such as the colour of soil in a ploughed field, where I had never thought of looking for beauty before. He taught me about the birds and animals and how to catch fish with my hands. I learned so much from him, but didn't appreciate it then. He could remember the old English queen coming to the throne.'

'Queen Victoria?'

'Aye. Hen Daid remembered his boyhood like it was yesterday. Many a wonderful tale he would paint for us children in Welsh, for English, the 'thin language' as he called it, was mostly beyond him - he only ever learned a few words in his long life. Hen Daid would say, some of us believe in God and some of us don't. Look around you, see our mountains, rivers and meadows. If you can't believe in the Almighty, believe in His works.

Jonathan stared up at the happy Welshman. 'Do you believe in God?'

'Yes.'

'Why, Taid? Because you go to Church?'

'No. I go once or twice a week to give my thanks for the things I have been given and to see my friends there.'

'Why aren't you angry with me for not believing in God?'

'Oh, because... he looked down and winked, 'because you are very young and I didn't have any faith until I grew to be a man.'

'Really, Taid?'

'Really, Jon Bach! But don't you go telling a soul.'

'Why didn't you believe, Taid?'

'For the same reasons as you...'

The boy looked up at the farmer silently and then into the panorama before them. Owain Williams knew Jonathan had asked his question with an open heart. He remembered times long ago when no one could talk such talk in a God-fearing land. He gave the bluntest answer he could.

'You are using only your head and haven't yet learned to use your heart wisely.'

The youngster stared and his grandfather smiled back.

'Your heart is your feelings - happiness - sadness - love - hate. Understand?'

He nodded.

'Too much heart and a man becomes open to the clever person who might trick him, pretending about things which are not true.'

'Lies.'

'Yes lies. A clever man, who does clever things by deceit and trickery to win his way in the world may gain many worldly things, but something of his spirit goes.' He looked down at the boy happily. 'I have lived for a long while now and still I cannot tell you what this thing is that is lost, but believe me, Jon Bach, something of great value does go from greedy men. It fades away from those who learn to smother natural kindness for their fellow creatures, given to us all at birth. We must love each other as best we may - and that could be the hardest commandment of all!'

They walked on, hand in hand now down the ffridd, the sun shining through a gap burned through high cloud. The Welshman indicated over to his right and the family climbed a stile at the side of the field, walking on through a more rugged terrain of gorse and heather, which ran alongside the ffridd. After a while Mr Williams stopped, taking the scene in silently. He looked out across a small meadow of the lushest green grass which was filled with late bluebells and wood anemones, they ran unhindered from his polished, dust-specked boots to a dry stone wall some fifty yards distance. The countryman's sharp eyes lifted towards a sparrowhawk hanging motionless on clever, fluttering wings high above in the mackerel sky. All the family followed Owain's eyes and watched. A broad growth of brambles, ferns and bracken had spread itself before the rugged wall, which turned away from them, lichen covered, to drop down into a small dell at the end of the meadow. Suddenly, the bird fell through the silent air towards its unseen prey like a dropped stone and vanished, terminating some small creature's life in cruel payment for its food. Owain looked at his two grandsons staring wide-eyed at the wall which hid the mean little death.

'This is still a beautiful world, in spite of nature's cruelties witnessed now and then. But perhaps the people of Wales have need to give their thanks more than most. That is why we love Church on Sunday morn, Jonathan, it is where we can sing God's praises as I have explained - for deep down, we Welsh know how lucky we are to have this land for our own. In life, learn to use your heart together with your head, fy yr , and you will grow to be a happy man. That is what I believe God wants from us all in the end, to be happy.'

Both boys were holding their grandfather's hand, William seeing the same powerful beauty he had all his life, his cousin learning fast. Taid Hafod joined in and said his piece about a marvellous old Welsh preacher he remembered as a youth, Reverend Hughes, and how he had watched great funeral corteges pass near his home in Llangernyw. The family moved on, a happy and expectant air rose as Ianto Jones' old stone farmhouse grew at the bottom of a sunny meadow above the dry stone wall. A customary large pot of tea, hot buttered scones and gossip with

Gwen's brother and his family was now only a few minutes away, the Pen y Rhiwlas climb had been thirsty work and their English service in St. Garmon's Church awaited them in little over half an hour. Owain Williams climbed onto an oaken stile straddling the ancient wall for the thousandth time. He held his hand out to Gwen and the others, feeling as happy as any man could. Soon they were all striding down the meadow, the boys playing tag and Owain opening the Jones' creaking kitchen door to a warm family welcome.

*     *     *

My first concern was for Jonathan. It was required of me to guide this ancient family taking care of him as I have explained. Owain Williams was the best of his kind and I had determined upon meeting this hardy man before his grandson arrived at Hendre Bach. Owain had seen me in the past, but only at a distance and in the half light of dusk. Will-o'-the-wisps are we. Inhabiting a body if needs drive. We are the Doorkeepers of your world.

Jonathan too was about see - or rather I should say sense my presence for the first time when he went to Church this day. I would join with Squire Bellamy, the leader of the little community as they all gave thanks and praise to Almighty God under the direction of Reverend Griffith. Rumour had it across the scattered population that it was the Squire who dressed up as if one of his long dead ancestors to ride the hills at night. Locals called the apparition Mad Silas – hardly daring to accept the probability that the wild figure thundering before the moon was their principled leader, always respected, if not revered as he stood before them to read the lesson each week. Their probability was close to the truth. I had inhabited the Squire's ageing body on a number of occasions to gain a little notoriety and establish myself as a spectral creature. I was justified in this as will be seen later. But the affluent Squire knew nothing of my benign possession of him, or at least he felt nothing palpable; yet some vague affectations had appeared of late suggesting something unusual may have occurred. I needed to take care, for possession can cause true madness if it is abused. I will not enter people who are troubled in spirit or mind – they have enough to bear. Every Doorkeeper is obliged by Mother Earth to select an appropriate host; a strong individual who will survive habitation for a short time in pursuance of Her wishes.

42

Bellamy was of this kind. Under my direction he had brought out old, foppish clothes secretly from a little used wing of his grand house, knowing nothing of what he was doing. Thus, wearing these extravagant, colourful garments we rode his great stallion across those hills at night. This was my talisman; an illusion of something to be feared, to mark me out as special and spiritual – an image of great importance for success.

The opportunity to meet Owain Williams came two weeks before Jonathan's arrival. We met near a wood he knew well called, Coed Cilcennus. I needed to produce an unexpected shock in a familiar place and this seemed perfect. At my direction Bellamy rode out from the wood with the inbred grace of a nobleman on his great white stallion. The lumbering wagon came to a halt, the big shire horse whinnying its surprise. Owain sat transfixed as I had hoped - a spectral confrontation before him in broad daylight, ten yards from that verdant wood he had played in as a boy. The Squire's stare held firm; shiny buckled shoes and dandy clothes from another age kept Owain Williams in a grip of iron and in those precious moments, as my host lifted a whitened hand and pointed a manicured finger, I captured Owain's spirit for a short while. The Welshman continued staring in horror right into the squire's wild, blue-grey eyes. The noble head was held high and proud; rouge at the cheeks, powdered hair lifting white as snow on a light breeze from under the tricorne hat –a flesh and blood ghost from centuries past. No one had been this close to the madman before and for brief moments Owain felt a kiss of terror among his confusion. This I knew and felt his pain.

Twists of smoke remained about the hill farmer's corn cob pipe, a stoic look now upon his weather-beaten face - which said much of the man. He was a Celt; built from powerful sinew and strong bones that came from an ancient line of humanity. Its generation on generation passage had handed on to each man and woman the ability to survive through strengths of body and mind that was quiet remarkable. This fortitude of flesh and spirit had run almost unbroken over ten thousand years of the humble Williams' clan. Behind Owain on the stilled wagon was a goodly supply of wet, black peat, taken that day from high up on the Hafod, at Fawnog-fawr. Celtic intuition from those centuries of natural selection burned with vigour in their hearts, not thinned yet by worldly progress. Their tough existence was accepted as normal life; to build a two mile long dry stone wall perhaps, or turn the rich, manmade soil in their vegetable gardens for the few hours left in a long day - land hard won and set in sheltered places among the thin earth and rock of the precarious mountains.

43

This challenging country remained the land of forefathers: Wales, a beautiful realm. But it could have been Scotland, or Ireland or Brittany. Or some far flung part of oldest Europe far away from urban communities. The Celts had lived in many places. They were a race apart.

Owain's big shire horse kept quite still, holding the farm wagon firm, and the world about us no longer held sway. He was mine briefly and I had to succeed in winning his heart to my undertakings. Soon warmth was on his cheek from an unexpected release of tears; it was followed by awareness which said, watch and listen. Memories rolled in and flooded. Pain surfaced in his stout heart. The terrible grief Jonathan's mother, Siân had brought upon her family when she was a young girl he had held down over those many years to keep hurt at bay. It came back in full in those moments.

By my wordless instruction Owain watched his only daughter; young, energetic and fiery in the dreamscape I had created around that wagon seat. Through it Siân told her family she was leaving them for good. And nothing they could do would stop her. I needed him to remember all; everything she had been to them, in this way he could learn to face and master the terrible pain inside. Such a route was the only way to win Owain's co-operation. And so it was. Powerful, vivid pictures of this girl leaving them long ago hurried his mind like driftwood before a huge wave. The wagon and the world around us became distant. I had grown to love this true countryman who was being won over at the commands of Mother Earth through me, yet he felt no awareness of events, or of my interaction with him. Soon things were in place for Siân's son, a new bright light thrown into their emotional darkness.

The peat laden wagon moved off to my command, rocking its way unhurriedly down the steep incline towards the farmhouse, Owain singing in his beautiful baritone voice with quiet pleasure as if nothing at all had happened. Squire Bellamy turned the big white stallion towards the wood at my silent instruction, his eyes glazed into oblivion whilst I saw all. In a few minutes Coed Cilcennus and the flower strewn meadow had returned to summer tranquillity. And so I moved forward once more, entering Ianto Jones' old stone farmhouse beside the Williams family, following them on their way to church this Sunday morn.

# Six

At nine forty-five a solitarily bell rang out clearly and its toll broke over the walls of St Garmon's Church like water. The sounds flowed quickly across grey slate roofs of the village and onto the surrounding countryside as if a dam had burst. Owain Williams looked up from an old kissing gate at the end of Ianto Jones's farm and smiled as its pealing prettied the otherwise silent air. He turned to Gwen as good-natured remarks were made on the time keeping qualities of the Churchwarden's old pocket watch, for Glyn Evans or his bell ringer were at least ten minutes early. The clock they normally relied on was being repaired, so Taid Hafod said. A narrow pathway led to the single road which ran through Capel Garmon village, everyone looked up towards the church then set off cheerfully in its direction.

Tall, black wrought iron gates were already open for Sunday services. From the entrance, a gentle grass path led up to the porch with a row of pollard yew trees on either side. The ten yews, actually looking like bushes had been cut by a woodsman who knew his craft, for each rounded form was wreathed, one to another, to create a high continuous guarding hedge on either side at a height of something like ten feet. The pollard trees were still young and wore dense, rich green foliage beneath new growths of yellow-green on the surface, leaving minimal space around the bottom for a small boy with a pea shooter. The shaded walkway extended a warm, peaceful entrance for the local parishioners who came regularly to venerate God and perhaps gain His comfort. Occasionally, a friendless traveller passing through and far from home may have been tempted to accept its gentle invitation, such peace seemed to linger about the place.

To the right of the gates stood a stone war memorial. Jones General's store was to the left. It had remained unchanged from the time when Jonathan's mother worked there as a young girl 14 years before, suddenly quitting his kind-hearted employ to work in service at the doctor's house in Belgravia Square, London. Jones General, old now with a badly ulcerated leg still ran the shop, although his wife had passed away some years since. The stone war memorial, enclosed by a small iron fence, was surmounted by a tall cross. Inscribed on the grey polished stone face of the obelisk were the names of fifteen dead Welsh soldiers who had fallen in the Great War, lost to the tiny parish for over thirteen years now. Fresh wild flowers smiled a colourful salute before the solemn remembrance, set in a brown vase set at the bottom.

Retired greengrocer, Bob Lloyd, known by everyone as Bob Bananas stood in the Church porch awaiting the ten o'clock congregation, his eyes shining brightly through thick bottle-glass spectacles. Bob, sidesman at St. Garmon's Church for many years, liked to greet people and give out the books as they went in but would say only two things to open up a conversation no matter what the week had done. If it was a nice day, Good morning. Fine day. If the weather was poor, Good morning. Thin wind.

He smiled his customary welcome at Mrs Hughes, a widow since the war as she made her way along the shaded path towards him. 'Good morning. Fine day, Mrs Hughes.'

'Indeed, Mr Lloyd.' Even now, after all these years her Sunday best looked like widow's weeds. She put her bible under her left arm and took the proffered hymn and prayer book.

Glyn Evans, Church warden and proud of it as a squireen, a worthy of the Parochial Church Council too, offered a customary smile from inside the door and bid her welcome. She would, in all probability, be the first of sixty souls accepting the call to worship this morning.

The village was filling with people now. Wagons pulled by shires, bachelors on horseback coming in from the surrounding farms, the majority on foot and everyone passing courteous, cheerful greetings on the bright, week-opening day. Men known well in yorks and hob-nailed boots had transformed themselves as well as hardship allowed, wife or sweetheart on their arm in best finery smiling happily, careful conversations, pleased that for a short while at least the work had ceased.

As Lord Webster's son walked beside his Taid, he watched the happy ritual and the people with some fascination, for this was the first time he had heard Welsh spoken in such a general way. Even though they were going to an English service, the language of Wales filled Capel Garmon like a hand in a glove.

A lank, secretive youth of about seventeen, with darkling staring eyes peered at him out of a shadowy cottage door, then, after some moments, he melted away slowly into the gloom like some apparition bent on mischief. Jonathan gaped and turned slowly as they passed the ivy clad doorway.

'Jacob Touch.' William put a finger to the side of his nose. 'My mam says to keep away.'

'Why?'

The Welsh boy looked surprised. 'Because he's touched. You know.' He tapped his head.

'Mad?'

46

'Stop that talk, you two, its nearly at the Church door we are.'

They chorused, 'Yes Nain,' and tried not to smirk.

One time Church sidesman, Thomas Henblas, came out of a doorway and offered greetings to the Williams family then strode away in front of them, the backside of his black serge suit trousers shining like a new penny piece as he lifted the jacket to adjust his braces. He raised his hat and gave gentle condolences to poor Jenny Davies who had lost her husband, Harry the week before. He was Thomas's long time drinking partner at the White Horse Inn, which stood opposite the Church gates. They had been good friends even though Harry Davies remained stubbornly English, rather like a Glaswegian who had settled in London for good. It caused good-natured jesting from some, but the fun never rankled him. He was boxed in his wooden suit now. Good cedarwood with best brass handles and a brass plate on the lid - all professionally attended to by Cadwaladr Jones, the undertaker in Llanrwst. They had planted him six feet down in the rich Welsh soil of the old Churchyard these three days past, but it was still a sorrowful thing, more even than simply dying. The effort of sending Harry Davis back to Reading in Berkshire would have cost a great deal, much too much for a widow on limited means. His only brother was dead.

Harry had loved living here, he worked in the Welsh hills for thirty four years, everything from cutting slate in Blaenau Ffestiniog to shepherding and foresting across the Conwy valley, he even spoke quite good Welsh and everyone said the views of the Snowdon range from his new plot behind the Church were particularly outstanding - pity he couldn't see them now, or perhaps he could. All in all they thought it best that Harry should remain there in Capel Garmon village with them, where he had become loved for himself.

Jonathan jumped when a small man, thin as a whippet, shot out of an alley to run in the opposite direction to everyone else. Dewi Lewis was dressed in the manner of an olden day farm servant with only his chin shaven, a red spotted handkerchief tied loosely around his neck. He pulled at it and started to undo a torn corduroy waistcoat whilst breaking into a run down the narrow street, then his sweat-stained woollen shirt came out of muddy corduroy trousers and people turned smiling; he twisted about, passing parishioners and offering hurried, friendly greetings to everyone for he knew them all, hob-nailed boots clattered loudly on the cobbles before an open doorway swallowed him.

'Old Lewis will make it just in time, he usually does...'

Gwen looked at her husband. 'That little man has been late for weeks now, Owain.'

The farmer shrugged his shoulders, unconcernedly.

'I know why, Nain!'

She looked down at William. 'You know?'

'You won't tell me off?'

'No.'

William pushed his dark curls back and grinned proudly at his cousin, having got the family's attention. 'Everyone's getting ready for Church on Sunday morn, including Evans gamekeeper, so Dewi Lewis does a spot of poaching whilst they're not looking. They say he's made a fine art of it too. Michael Irish at school has seen him sneaking back with a salmon like you've never seen. Dewi's up at four o'clock to be ready for dawn and the rising of game fish - and there's pheasants as well and...'

'That's enough of that, William.' Taid looked angrily at him for a moment and lifted his cap to Mrs Owens Baker as she walked briskly past the family, her fixed courtesy smile displayed on thin, pale lips, her pointed nose still just slightly uplifted as if avoiding something unpleasant in the gutter beneath their feet. A normal response from Mrs Owens Baker unfortunately, even in return to Owain's polite, large toothy smile which he offered to everyone without any reservations.

'If that woman has heard what you have just said it'll be around the village in an hour.'

A queue had formed along the path to the Church porch by the time the Williamses arrived. Old Bob Bananas stood slightly stooped at the porch door, his white, once sandy hair brushed back stiffly and coloured like snow, his friendly eyes, framed by the thick bottle-glass spectacles were full of pleasure at seeing old friends and neighbouring farmers, most of whom he had know all of his life. Owain Williams chatted briefly when his turn came to collect hymn and prayer books, Gwen at his side, Megan, the boys with Nain and Taid Hafod directly behind, yet the sidesman gave the same careful time to them all as with everyone else there; a gentle, slightly intense manner about him, as if any subject raised was automatically worthy of the fullest consideration.

The men removed their hats as they entered, Megan and Nain fussing the boys with whispered entreaties to William in particular to show everyone how well he could behave. Many of the congregation were in their set places already, the same position each week, like Owain Williams, many paid the Church half-a-crown a year for the privilege of having their own pew. The family dropped to their knees in silence to offer personal prayers, as were others members of the congregation. Jonathan copied them, and after a few moments eased one eye open and peeked a look at William. Mr Williams had wisely placed each grandson on either side of him for some form of control. William's eyes were screwed tightly shut, the English boy assumed he was praying for the vicar to fall off the pulpit steps or the organ to go bang or something and took the opportunity to look around carefully, but before he could the family finished their devotions and sat back on the hard wooden pew quietly. They were sitting to the left of the aisle, about halfway down and it was quite crowded there. Jonathan noticed people looking at him, friendly but nosey. He remembered his cousin's words...when it comes to neighbours, the Welsh are very stitched up, 'till they know you that is... He stared about. There were smells of mothballs, polished oak and dubbined boots all around him, he wanted to go to the toilet but was scared stiff to mention it to Taid. Behind the pulpit was a stained glass window depicting Saint George killing the dragon. Sunshine outside had lit the coloured glass and it looked lovely, reminding him of home.

Suddenly, he felt William's outstretched finger tap his leg. He turned, Taid had his head in the prayer book and the boy indicated to the porch and whispered. The sound of the squire's family carriage pulling up outside was distinct in the silent Church. The two looked at each other.

'Don't worry. Old Silas is fast asleep inside Squire now. He comes out at night. I'll show you him soon!'

Taid looked over the top of the prayer book. 'Be quiet now, or it'll be the worst for you.' He glared at the pair of them and William moved back quickly onto his seat as Jonathan remembered tales of a madman who roamed the hills and forests on a big white horse. Soon muffled words could be heard outside and Squire Bellamy walked in grandly with his wife on his arm, their three daughters gliding quietly behind. Two were in long, sumptuous old-fashioned dresses like eighteenth century ladies, the third and youngest, at about Jonathan's age, was dressed more plainly and staring shyly at the floor. Two other visiting members of the gentry, a man and woman having the appearance of Edwardian well-to-dos, brought up the rear. If any whispers had been among the congregation beforehand, they were silenced now. The party started down the aisle like minor royalty, the swish of the ladies silk clothes, the pad of best Parisian leather shoes on the flagstones. Suddenly Squire Bellamy was looking straight at Jonathan, it wasn't an inquisitive stare, or any kind of stare at all really, just a gentle look from someone seeing a stranger among the familiar. The gentry passed by to take their places at the very front of the nave, directly before the lectern, on which was inscribed the assurance, *The word was with God and the word was God.*

The English boy looked around the now full congregation of nearly seventy people; at their faces, their clothes, their smiles, he knew only a few, mainly by word of mouth, the majority were complete strangers. Most looked happy - happy to not be working he thought - some faces were noncommittal and a few dismal in appearance, but every man, woman and child had done their level best to look Sunday dressed. Squire Bellamy, Lord of the Manor and his family, Doctor Kemp who sat directly behind the squire, Mr Cartwright, inn keeper, Jones General, shop keeper, Meurig Evans, gamekeeper from Cefn Rhydd Estate, many tenant farmers and their families, men and womenfolk little more than peasants and a scattering of farm servants and labourers. It was said that a Sunday service in a country Church contained more human smells under one roof at the same time that could be found anywhere, notwithstanding the infirmary, whose medical odours obliterated most everything.

As the gentry seated themselves at the long front pew, Reverend Griffith's familiar face peered around the vestry door, his long grey sideburns standing out like a Victorian gentleman farmer. Jonathan recognised him immediately. This was the vicar who had directed Lady Denham Hope's big Rolls Royce motorcar to Hendre Bach farm from the front passenger seat nearly a month ago, when Aunt Eleanor had brought him to Wales. Griffith's greying head returned back inside the vestry, the organist started playing the hymn, *See the Destined Day Arise* and everyone got to their feet. There was no choir to lead the way, or stalls should one ever be formed. After about a minute of energetic organ playing by Mrs Griffith, the country vicar made his way alone solemnly towards the chancel and Taid took the opportunity to speak careful, whispered directions to the boys, calling for proper behaviour throughout the service. The congregation watched familiar steps taken into the stepless chancel, familiar steps before the altar. Reverend Griffith's slight dip of his head signalled everybody to kneel.

*The Table at the Communion-time having a fair white linen cloth upon it, shall stand in the Body of the Church, or in the Chancel, where Morning and Evening Prayer are appointed to be said. And the Priest standing at the north side of the Table shall say the Lord's Prayer, with the Collect following, the people kneeling.*

Jonathan should have learned the Lord's Prayer at his mother's knee, in fact Siân was always too busy for him and his nanny for a short time, Mrs Stone taught him his catechism. He found himself saying the Lord's Prayer word perfect for the first time in many years and peeked a second look at William who was picking his nose, but doing a manful job of the Prayer nonetheless for that. Taid Hafod had his eyes tightly shut, there was a drip forming on the end of his nose, and Auntie Megan looked as if she wanted the toilet as badly as he did, her face had a pulled look which he guessed must be on his. Reverend Griffith finished the Collect and was on the third of the Ten Commandments, with the congregation's responses returning strongly, when Jonathan's inquisitiveness overcame his forced politeness and he found himself staring at Nain carefully and then his grandfather. To the lad's shock, Taid lifted one canny eye, it was as if the old Welshman had been looking at him all the while through closed lids. Eyes widened, eyeball confronted eyeball for a split-second and the unexpected shock of being caught ignoring the service flattened Jonathan's prying curiosity completely. Thereafter, he made some effort to follow high points of the liturgy, if only to keep himself out of any further trouble. But he couldn't help drifting.

It seemed as if he was doing two things at once. The congregation and family were rather faint all about now, mouthing words. Taid must be pleased with him he thought. At the same time he could see outside the Church as clear and as natural as could be. It gave him the same feeling as when he saw his father's face in Nain's back kitchen. A special, good feeling like a gift unexpected in the week. The shop and war memorial looked a little different, Taid or someone must know what he was doing but they didn't take any notice. And then they got fainter. A soldier limping with a stick crossed the road to his right. The little window in his mind scared him now, but he grasped hard at the image, knowing that he was going to see his mother from long ago.

\*     \*     \*

The sun came out from heavy rain filled clouds scudding over St. Garmon's Church. Next door, old Mrs Cadwallader stood outside Mr Jones' general store, looking at the dark rolling shadows climbing up the steep green slope of Pen y Rhiwlas opposite. It was three and a half miles over that hill to Hendre Bach and probably raining before Siân got in. But this was the last time. The very last. The old lady was sure of that now. London it was, do her good she thought. Still a long way for a child to go and start in service from scratch. She turned and walked down the cobbled street, leaning on her bamboo cane as she went, leaving the little village to silence.

51

Then a wispy girl, slight and nimble stepped out of the general stores, the one the old lady had been musing on, she moved onto the veranda porch, pulling the shop door shut carefully and in doing so, woke the tinkling bell which had filled her day so often; hazel eyes bright, auburn hair turning golden as the sun came out. She put her hat on, a brown felt thing with a turned up brim, certain to look hideous, although no one ever noticed. She retrieved her brown paper parcel from a wicker chair outside the door. It had sheltered under the store's coloured glass canopy for years and was where Nain Cadwallader sat most evenings until Jones General sent her on her way home, gentle as you like, with a reminder that the chair was for customers, really.

A magpie screeched among overgrown branches of a yew in the graveyard and flew over the Church roof and then down, followed by its mate, black and white flutterings rising and falling around the east window - some more screechings, then gone. Fly away magpies before Evans game keeper sees you and hangs you on squire's gate, so all can see that he is doing his job this year too. The birds reappeared suddenly and vanished with equal speed behind the White Horse Inn on the other side of the road.

'Good luck for someone!'

She hadn't really heard the tinkling door, such were her thoughts.

'Two they say, you see. Two's lucky, for some.' Jones General smiled. He was slightly red faced. Always got like that when talking to women on his own.

She turned around and looked up at him, his pork chop sideburns, fat kindly face, flour covering the apron around his huge girth and more flour up his forearms. 'Perhaps it's some luck for me?' she offered.

He smiled more, showing new false teeth. 'For you? Yes. Perhaps it is. We wish you luck from the magpies! Have you told your Mam and Dad?'

She did up the top button of her wool mixture coat, new two years since from the big clothes shop in Llanrwst. 'No, Mr Jones. I haven't been home for two weeks. You know that.'

He nodded, knowing she had missed Church too. The strong sort of nods he specialised in when customers asserted their rights. And his eyes took on their stern, fatherly look. 'Do they know you were trying for work in service all the way down in London? Now a big girl like you, sixteen an' some,' he rubbed the flour from his hands and it clouded over to the Church gates on the breeze, 'a lady almost you are;

52

well me an' Mrs Jones, we said nothing when the first letter came an' we've said nothing since...'

Siân's face hardened. 'Nothing to Mam or Dad, or anyone?'

Jones General shook his head and looked up and down the empty street. 'It's none of my business - but you should tell them, young lady!'

The girl smiled. It was her best smile. She had practised in front of the small mirror in her attic room above the shop where she had lodged for two years. It was a good smile. She could even turn men's heads with it. She really found out in Llanrwst a year ago come high summer when Mam and Dad had taken her shopping and two weeks after the war took sweet Emrys Evans, who had sparked her whilst he was on leave. She had learned since. Men liked her smile, the few young men left, those not at the Front, and the way she spoke to them. They looked at her legs too...

'Shouldn't you, Siân?'

'Yes. I'll tell them tonight, I promise, Mr Jones. That's why I'm going home, particular.' She smiled her special smile to win. 'I'm off on Monday on a train to start at a big house in Belgravia Square...'

Jones General opened his fat arms and she ran into his huge embrace. He looked down. 'You take care now. You hear what old Mr Jones says?'

She pulled away, straightening the flattened brown parcel, and nodded.

He looked at the sky as the sun went in. 'Looks like rain, girl. Tell Mam and Dad we'll miss you. Say me an' Mrs Jones wish you well.' He stood for a moment, fat hands on fat hips, then turned and the door bell tinkled behind him.

She looked down the street for the last time. Grey stone terraced walls, some lime washed and flaking now, the White Horse Inn with Mrs Roberts on the step of the saloon bar with a bucket and a scrubbing brush. Old Mr Owen, the horse doctor and herbalist was wandering down the street to Chapel at the other end of the village. No one else.

Good bye Capel Garmon. You've had sixteen of my years, you'll have no more. She walked over to the Church gates and looked through them to the porch, then along beside the wall to where the road turned. She peered through new green growth on the bushes to stone heads either side of the east window, a man and woman. They said it was old Queen Victoria and the Bishop of St Asaph. Goodbye Church.

The kissing gate squeaked by Uncle Ianto's farm as she passed through to the path which ran up through the hendre onto the steep

53

lower slopes of Pen y Rhiwlas. Uncle Ianto's farm was where they stayed for lunch after Church on Sunday morn, waiting for Sunday school in the afternoon, then back home again after Evensong. Dad sometimes skipped Sunday school for the animals and they walked home just with Mam. A round trip of seven miles from Hendre Bach over the Rhiwlas, walking a thousand feet down to Capel Garmon in rubber boots carrying your best shoes all polished and shiny in a shopping bag ready for Church, and then a thousand feet up again.

Jonathan's mother never walked there again.

Jon Bach jumped as the congregation rose for *Jesus Shall Reign Where'er the Sun*. They were all filling his senses once again. He had seen his mother leaving *Capel Garmon* at a time long past – before he was born – whilst everyone else had been following the service and he didn't know what to do. The little window of perception in his head had closed. Was gone. Had vanished completely. He realised that he was sweating badly, as if running wild down the Rhiwlas with William.

It was soon after, just before the prayer had started for the Almighty to rule the heart of King George that Jonathan saw Squire Bellamy turn away from the vicar and look straight at him once again, eyes shinning brightly in the candlelight. William's story about Mad Silas froze within him.

## Seven

Jonathan said nothing of his supernatural experience in Church to the family. He knew what had happened in his head was right. Special. Just for him. But the little refuge from far away Croydon town knew nothing more.

On the following Tuesday Jon Bach and William left Hafod cottage as they had found it, except for some herbs freshly picked for Nain Hafod and soon the lanky figure of William was leading a way across the rocky plateaux and back down the hafod slopes. Jonathan had kept his feelings about Squire Bellamy to himself. This was all new and he was still very keen to show himself to his cousin in the best possible light. No cissy talk of being frightened by stories of Mad Silas, whom he had now discovered from William was also the Squire dressed up. Most in the area had heard whisperings about Silas riding a big white horse at night, him clothed as an old fashioned aristocrat in a long tailed coat, tricorne hat and blunderbuss gun, hunting for Frenchies - whoever they were. He sounded mad as a hatter. When their eyes had met in Church, Squire looked every bit the leader of the little community, someone to be respected, looked up to: safe. And everyone in that church, bursting as it was to the seams, treated him with real deference. Yet Jonathan Webster at only ten years of age sensed something odd about their short unspoken contact, as if the man had some strange insight into what a mere boy was just beginning to feel for himself. This ancient land had an enormous soul of its own which civilised Croydon, or any other urban world could never have dreamed existed, and somehow Jonathan knew it wanted to communicate with him. His Celtic blood was running fast now, faithful hands from the mists of time were drawing him on.

They skirted the farmhouse by running through Cae Bach field and dropped down a steep grassy slope which led onto the Llanrwst to Nebo road. Dinner was nearly three hours off and such precious free time was not to be wasted for a second - William would see to that.

On the other side of the road, beyond a great moss encrusted wall, ancient, secluded woodland dropped away steeply. Even though the boys had run for the most part down from the hafod, through the hendre and were now working further down into the Conwy Valley itself, the wood before them was no nearer civilisation, remaining miles from house, settlement or shop - deep in the heart of Welsh countryside. But it was warmer here too. Lowlands. A different world to explore.

'Over this wall is Squire's land. He doesn't bother with this part at all. We'll go along to the river, then follow it down to Squire's Wood, proper - and that's a different matter. Gentry don't like you in there, lad. It's flogging or worse ifn you're caught!'

They climbed the wall and dropped down a steep overgrown bank into dank, tangled fauna. Except for elm, ash and some oaks near the road, the hand of man had never touched this remote wooded place - only a boy, and his great grandmother were its occasional visitors for the collection of nature's bounty - a steep, verdant greenwood, primeval Britain just as it had been over 5,000 years before them. The boys stood up and worked their way along the lush slope strewn with bluebells and lesser celandine, two trespassers staring about cautiously as they walked towards the bottom of the bank. Blackbird, song thrush and woodland linnet sung their quiet joy at a distance, then the sudden, urgent warning twitter of the blackie lifted across the lush woodland floor as she saw them. Ancient oaks, flourished there far from the road, all holding their great limbs proudly towards the sky - these were the unbroken descendants of the first trees ever to grow in that place. The boys started to move deeper into the thicket, William pointing and telling.

'Look lively, Jonathan!'

The English lad was suddenly feeling very homesick. He thought about his mother deserting him and his father's brave attempt to save them by seeking his fortune in America. The ten-year-old speeded up as William darted ahead, running and jumping obstacles like Tomos the hare under sun-dappled canopies above. Jonathan caught him standing by a thick clump of elm where the sun was able to shine through a break in the branches high overhead.

'Soapwort.' The farm boy pointed to a tall, pink flowering plant with long flowing green leaves. They stooped to their haunches. 'One of the weeds we collect for Nain Hafod, they're usually nearer the road. If you pour boiling water on the green parts it makes a lather-water we use for cleaning wool and washing woollen clothes in.' He picked a leaf and handed it to Jonathan. 'You can use it for washing yourself too, if money gets short and you run out of soap.'

Jonathan wrinkled his nose. 'Do you run out of soap?'

'Sometimes. Aye. They do say that the lather is good for washing invalid's hair, or folk's who's going bald. The leaves and roots are poisonous though, but Nain Hafod makes many remedies from them for gout, rheumatism and skin diseases.' He stood up and started running again, making a twisting route through the pathless wood. They came to a wide patch of bilberries which made a mauve backdrop to the lush fauna. 'My Mam and Nain at Hendre farmhouse make jam with these, I bring in loads and Mam sells the jam at the market in Llanrwst.'

He pointed to fattening berries covered in their white powdery bloom, 'but they're not ready yet.'

The steepness of the incline had eased, and as the boys walked further into the copse, trees, bushes and abundant plant life grew ever more dense. William, clearly at home in the wilderness, looked back at his cousin. 'No one ever comes here, Jonathan - ever! If you were on your own and broke a leg or something - so couldn't walk back home - you'd become old bones here and still not be found!'

They stopped, both leaning their backs against a big ash tree. William took out a pocket knife, unfolded a long sharp blade with practised care and started to cut a piece of bark from the trunk. 'Five years ago, Dafydd Ellis, the chapel preacher's nephew broke his ankle in a dingle. His twelfth birthday it was in a few days. He was a farm boy down on Cwm farm, about five or six miles from here. Hurrying back home was poor Dafydd, the weather had closed in and it was getting dark. Weather can change like that in the hills,' William snapped his fingers dramatically, 'and when they found him next day Dafydd Ellis was stiff as a board - he had frozen to death!'

The English lad looked shocked.

'Oh, you'll be alright, Jon. Do as I tell you an' you'll be fine.' He grinned cheekily. 'It's summer now, anyway. Put that old piece of bark in your pocket and give it to Nain Hafod when you meet her. She'll be pleased.' He turned to go and then looked back. 'C'mon then.'

'What's special about this bit of tree?'

'It's bark from an ash tree.'

'So?'

William put his hands on his slim hips, a friendly but barely patient smile spread thinly on his lips. 'Don't you English know anything, Jon?'

Jonathan folded his arms, didn't anger, and made a guess. 'You use it to scrub wool with that soapwort weed back there.'

William burst out laughing, he rolled backwards and forwards with such mirth that Jonathan, initially taken aback, could not help but start laughing too. They slid down the tree, backs against the trunk, legs out across the grass, their sides beginning to ache from the effort and then collapsed on the ground in convulsions of uncontrollable laughter.

Jonathan took a breath. 'It's for lighting fires which keep going out?'

More uncontrollable mirth.

'No, no... You'd best stick close to me, for the time being, until you get to learn some lore.'

They sat up rubbing their eyes. Jonathan took out his neatly folded handkerchief, opened it and wiped his face and eyes. 'Lore?'

'Aye. Lore.'

They sat quietly for a few moments. 'Like the lore saying that the old piece of tree you've got in your pocket can cure a man who's sick through eating poor food. Lore which says...' the Welsh boy stood up, 'well a lot of things...' He looked up through the green canopy at the sun and turned to Jonathan. 'Day's travelling on. We'd best be on our way.' The strong brown hand was offered and Jonathan was pulled to his feet. In the far distance a train's steam-whistle sounded way off through the trees. 'Hear that?'

Jonathan nodded, brushed his trousers energetically and felt his eyes start to water as he thought of it carrying him home to Surrey.

'That's a train running to Betws-y-Coed from Llandudno Junction. She runs the valley floor by the Conwy River,' William pulled up two long pieces of grass, started chewing one and offered the other as they moved on, the farm boy unaware of his young friends closeness to tears and Jonathan manfully checking them. Soon the sound of water rushing cheerfully over unseen rocks some distance ahead filled the woodland. William led the way through an expanse of harts tongue ferns, bracken, ragwort and brambles. He looked back, eyes bright.

'The river. It's seldom that you can hear her from the road, for she's well hidden in these deep wooded glens. The squire might have lawful ownership, but she's mine and Nain Hafod's. No one comes here but us. This wood is too remote for the gentry and too hard for the common farmers' sons.' He threw a strange glance at Jonathan. 'It's a magic place, Jon. Our secret. Keep faith with me and I'll show you something which only God and Old Mad Silas know is here...'

The English boy was perspiring now. Lines of sweat were trickling down his nose and the freckle-face looked as if it had been varnished. 'Who's Old Silas?'

'You look all in. For a townee, Jon Bach, you haven't done bad.'

Jonathan caught his cousin up. 'I'll do. Who's Old Silas really, then? You said he's the Squire dressed up!'

'That's for later. You look lively now, or we'll not make it there and back before supper.'

'Where we going?'

'You'll see...'

Fifty yards brought them through dense foliage to a deep gulley. The sides fell very steeply for the best part of sixty feet, and at its bottom a wonderful stream danced and roared into a deep blue pool. The gurgling rush of water over rocks and stones, sudden movement from two kingfishers skimming about the pool, then the briefest blue flashes before they vanished had little Jonathan Webster spellbound. Neolithic man returning to this gorge would have found no change at all. He would still be able to forage for wild berries, small fish and animals, for all were surviving there in abundance still - yet he had long since vanished from the face of the earth. The banks of the gulley were awash with bracken and other ferns, the boys made their way down carefully, holding onto rocks and anything which came to hand as the earth underfoot became progressively more slippery. Suddenly, when over halfway down, William indicated for Jonathan to keep quiet and both boys lowered themselves into the fern cover.

'Look on the far side of the pool, there's a family of otters.'

His whispered words highlighted the drama as the English townee peered carefully down the twenty feet of incline towards the beautiful slate bottomed blue pool.

'Stay here for a bit - if we move down any more they'll be scared away...'

And so the two friends watched the creatures gambol and play in the shaft of sunshine which lit the bubbling stream on its way through the ancient woodland; narrow, ethereal lines of rainbow coloured light fingered through the contrasting dull backdrop of trees behind the pool, beautifying an idyll to the level of magic.

Jonathan had never seen an otter close to before. Two large adults and three cubs were apparently completely unaware of their presence. A rocky shelf under a large gorse bush on the other side of the pool gave them space to lie in the sun, preen and play. They had lovely sleek grey-brown coats, flattened heads with broad muzzles and long whiskers like a seal he had seen in a zoo. The bitch dived and swam with her cubs as if enjoyment of life was her only purpose, whilst the big dog otter lay on his side and preened for a short while, stout tail and webbed feet moving as he rolled about nimbly. Suddenly he dived into the water making hardly a ripple and joined in their games; then the cubs climbed out onto the rock shelf under the overhanging gorse bush, this promoted new games which started the parents involvements afresh.

The two cousins sat watching for nearly fifteen minutes, exchanging occasional glances of mutual pleasure. From nowhere came a bark like a dog, then a weird scream. In an instant the family had dived down into the pool leaving the surface like glass and Jonathan felt ice tingling at his neck.

'What was that, William?'

'Fox calling his vixen, I think. Then her reply.' He looked at the English boy, his broad Celtic features moulded into puzzlement. 'Strange. They normally hunt singly - and then at night...' He stood up. 'Wait here. I'll go down and have a look.'

The dingle, Jonathan realised as he sat watching William, had suddenly fallen into a deep silence immediately after the otters had so amazingly vanished. Everything had changed in an instant. Birdsong and other sounds which had not really been registering in his mind were now stilled. The change was very marked. It was eerie. William reached the bottom of the slope and looked about. Then he jumped over the stream where it left the crystal pool, disappearing into the vegetation and trees on the other side in seconds.

The eerie silence seemed to go on for a long while although perhaps only minutes passed. Once, Jonathan thought he heard the bark again, but it was in the distance and he was unsure. Just before William returned, rooks started screaming at the tops of their tall trees beyond the glen. It seemed to signal a return, the place came alive again, but of the otters there was now no trace. Jonathan made his way down through the bracken to meet the Welsh boy by the pool.

'No sign of anything.' He looked about. 'Sure that was a vixen's scream, though. She's gone now.' He pointed to the leaf canopy around the stream. 'They know.' The birds were on full song as if nothing had happened to spoil the otter's play or their peace.

'Where have the otters gone?'

William stalked carefully along by the pool. Then he pointed across to the bottom of the fern bank. 'Look. See the flattened grass,' he whispered, 'that's where they got out and moved downstream.'

'They're gone?'

'Yes.' The boy signalled quiet.

'Are there any fish in here?'

He nodded. Together they moved stealthily to the side of the pool, lay down carefully on their stomachs and peered into the deep, cool depth. The water was so clear that they could see seven or eight feet down to crags of blue-grey slate at the bottom which gave the crystal clear water its beautiful hue. Across the floor of rippling colours, bright stones were taking Jonathan's eye when a shoal of rainbow trout flashed away towards some shelter downstream, near the end of the pool.

'Fishes!'

The older boy indicated with a finger to his lips. 'Trout. Some nice beggars in here. Sometimes I take one or two when the mood or some hunger takes.'

'You bring a rod down here?'

William smiled that friendly, slightly aloof smile. 'No, Jon. Just these.' He held up his hands.

The English lad's dark eyes nearly popped. 'You catch fish just with your bare hands?'

'Aye.'

'How?'

William rolled up his sleeves carefully and leaned over the pool. 'I slowly put my hands into the water like this....' he lowered his sinewy arms down through the clear water to a flat rocky outcrop about twenty inches below the surface and then turned his head slowly to look into the fascinated freckle-face of his young friend, 'then I look into the water and let my fingers search carefully about the stones for trout to be tickled and raised. Mister Trout loves his naps on this sunny shelf and a gentle tickle from me rarely goes amiss.'

Jonathan could hardly contain his excitement, 'Can we tickle one now?'

'No. It is never good to waste food. We have a distance to travel yet and there's nowhere to carry a nice fish home. When I am down here normally, it's for collecting herbs an' such for Nain Hafod, so a pair of trout can be slipped in a knapsack easy enough.' He got up and pointed downstream. 'C'mon, let's be on our way.'

They walked to the end of the lovely blue pool and looked over the end where the water overflowed down a magnificent waterfall.

'I love this place, Jon. Could never leave these hills and mountains and live in a city.' They looked ahead to a tangle of intertwining branches crossing the stream above the waterfall, it was covered with old man's beard, the woody climbing stems and sprays of greeny-white flowers smelling sweetly of vanilla on the gentle breeze. To the left, on the opposite side to which they had climbed down, foxgloves and a profusion of harebells were spread high up the steeply rising bank to reach larch and silver birch trees high above them. These fronted the more ancient trees of the silently brooding thickets which followed the stream all the way down to Squire's Wood. William turned to his confidant. 'Nain Hafod says woodland sprites live in this place for sure, and you can hear their happy laughter as the stream skips over stones and swings around the bends.'

The boys moved on down the gorge, keeping as close as they could to the sides of the stream. They drank from the crystal clear waters with cupped hands, ran games of tag and jumped the narrower parts to prove their mettle. Jonathan had come up considerably in the older boy's eyes. He was clearly Saesneg - English - and from a big town too, but he could stick pretty close to William wherever he went and that was good enough to win his respect.

'They say that nymphs and fairies live over there by the brook.' The Welsh farm boy pointed ahead to a small pool fed by the stream. It was not so grand as the one the otters had frequented but of enough size to cause interest.

'Fairies?' Jonathan wrinkled his nose, looked scornful and threw a stone downstream.

'Sure. Do you not believe in things of the secret world? Taid Hafod knows much of such things, so much it'd make your hair curl. He told me about the water nymphs. Over there, see the white stone near the side of the brook?' William's long forefinger indicated, his face suddenly intense, 'he came here once a long, long time ago and saw her there, sitting bold as you like, wings like a giant bumble bee and beautiful hair decked with tiny daisies that glowed in the sun.'

Jonathan stopped searching for another stone, pulled his hand out of the cold frothing water and glared.

'You don't believe me, do you?'

The English lad shrugged, wrinkled his nose again then caught sight of a pebble to his fancy and pulled it out.

'We're all the same really. Saesneg or Welsh folk. Everyone in the world, see. That's what both my Taids say. Only difference is that some of us lives in cities and some of us lives closer to the earth and right under the sky - whatever she might drop down on us - and we find the way to continue. Town folk like you have forgotten, that's all, an' we haven't.'

Jonathan looked intensely at his new friend. 'Forgotten what?'

'The other world, boy. The other world, see. Fair play to him, my Uncle Emyr knew all about the lores and the little folk as he called them. Came from South Wales did Uncle Emyr and told me all sorts, even though he wasn't really from around here. Nain Hafod knows about their ways too, but she doesn't say much about it now, not since Uncle Emyr crossed over these two summers past. He was her only brother and they were split up as children. Buried down at Melin-y-Coed Church he is and Nain Hafod puts flowers on his grave every month regular.'

Jonathan threw his stone and it dropped perfectly right against the white stone in the little pool. His dark eyes caught the Welsh boy's for a second before he looked away self-consciously. 'Has this stream got a name?'

William burst out laughing. 'On yes, she's got a name alright. Afon Gallt-y-Gwg.' He looked strangely at his young friend. 'In English that means River of the Angry Hill. And I know how she got that name!'

Jonathan knew his companion well enough by now and bad humour at being told stories full of fairies as if he was a baby, suddenly overflowed. 'Sounds a pretty stupid name to me, William!'

The Welsh lad said nothing, got up from the bank and without showing any hurt, knelt down and cupped his hands into the rushing water. 'You want another drink? *Nant* water is from the hills and is the cleanest anywhere. They do say that if a foreigner drinks from a Welsh mountain stream he will always return to Wales.'

William started to drink and slowly his young friend knelt down beside him and dipped his hands into the bubbling current.

Soon they were on their way again. The stream's fast flow increasing as they made their way through tall ferns, ancient weeds and prolific plant growth of all kinds. The way dropped suddenly into a narrow defile made by huge moss and lichen covered boulders which were both slippery and very hard to negotiate. The boys didn't talk, such was the noise from the roaring torrent. Beyond it, the stream settled to peace and meandered through a tiny untouched meadow. Buttercups littered the scene and the streams edge was populated with alders and willow trees.

'I come down here sometimes for salix. That's my mam's name for osiers.' William walked across to a row of lovely weeping willows and pointed to some new shoots. 'She makes nice strong baskets with these and sells them at the market.'

Jonathan appeared to have cheered up a little and the farm boy walked back to him, that friendly, slightly aloof smile flicking about his lips.

'I promised to tell you a secret about Squire Bellamy and his land didn't I?'

The younger boy nodded, but he wanted one question to be answered at a time. 'William, are there really water sprites and things living down here?'

'You're worried aren't you, Jon?'

Jonathan shrugged.

'They won't hurt you...'

The boy kicked at a clump of grass and looked warily at his new friend. 'Yes, but is there really a secret world, have you seen strange things down here?'

William stared, then pushed his hands deep into the pockets of his short ragged trousers. 'I've seen odd things. Aye. Can't be as certain as Uncle Emyr, though.   And Taid says to me, who knows what the world has hidden from men?'

Jonathan pulled a piece of bramble from his tweed jacket which was now looking a little worse for wear.  His face lit up as if suddenly, he had come to terms with the chance of encountering hob goblins and decided the risks were well worth taking.  'You really have got a secret, haven't you?'

The Welsh lad stared for a moment.  'Only if you keep faith with me.'

'What does that mean?'

'You must tell no one.  On the pain of death.'

'On the pain of death?'

'Aye.'

'On pain of death. then.'  His father's love of the unknown was with him already.  An adventurous spirit burned fiercely in Jonathan's character, set there by nature when she had made him with loving care.  In genuine innocence, twelve year-old William could not have said a better thing if he had wanted a real comrade to aid his wildest exploits.

William Williams nodded.  Behind them was an alder tree with a long, thick branch hanging lazily out over the stream.

'C'mon, Jon.  Look lively then, get up here and I'll tell you a little.'

He climbed up, Jonathan followed and within seconds they were both settled comfortably out over the clear water, muddy shoes swinging just above the gently wandering old stream.

'You've heard of the Ancient Romans?'

'Yes.'

'There was a big battle near this spot between Roman soldiers and the Celts, people who lived here thousands of years ago.  He watched his English friend's mouth open.  'There's something up there still, about half a mile away in Squire's Wood...'

Jonathan's eyes fairly glowed now.  'Really?'

'Sure, I found it!'  William looked up at the sky as if reconsidering his frankness, levered himself up onto the sturdy branch and jumped back down to the riverbank.  'Time's running by and chores must be done for Nain.'

Jonathan remained on the branch, his face reverential, then he turned angrily.  'That's not fair!'

'Come on, we've got to go.'

Jonathan wrinkled his nose. 'I want to see this thing.' He looked pleadingly at his new friend. 'Go on, William, it's only half a mile from here - you said so yourself.'

The benevolent smile vanished. 'Haven't you heard any of the things I've been telling you these weeks past, Jon Bach? It's dangerous. I mean it. I'll tell you more when we have time. Now come on.' He looked back, darkling eyes aglow. 'If you prove yourself and keep faith with me, I'll take you there soon - I promise.'

The English boy grinned for a moment then gritted his teeth, clenched his fists, freckle-face reddening by the second as William ran back alongside the gurgling stream with athletic ease, curly black hair bobbing. Just before he disappeared, Jonathan leapt from the old branch in open rage, yelling his friend's name and darted back along the riverbank before William could get from his sight.

# Eight

Lord you have been our refuge:
from one generation to another.
Before the mountains were born
or the earth and the world were brought to be:
from eternity to eternity you are God.
You turn man back into dust:
saying 'Return to dust you sons of Adam.'
For a thousand years in your sight are like yesterday passing:
or like one watch of the night.


Rain was hard falling in the pitch black night and pounding on the old slate roof, driving lines of spray off the eaves not far above the heads of the two boys as they lay fast asleep that night. Jonathan was completely unaware of Deldramena. Only aware of looking up at a lady holding his hand. She was very beautiful. Her eyes seemed to be on fire, golden eyes, burning with life. She had white flowers laced into her dark black hair and a cascading white robe about golden slippers, each step she took seemed to be barely touching the long sward of grass they were climbing, the greenest grass the boy had ever seen. The hill was crowned with seven tall *carialds*, tapering pillars of clear crystal. Each had four sides, each side glowed as if some facet of a huge precious stone. The lady led the boy forward, soon they were inside the great circle and walking towards a man standing at its centre who was dressed in long flowing raiment of white with a blue girdle at his waist upon which red letters were fashioned and devices he did not know. A show of dark leather about his shoulders was shaped like armour and upon his head a proud circlet helm shining it seemed with the last rays of sun upon the sea.

As they walked in silence Jonathan looked about to see distant hills, mountains and valleys, but crowded in every direction, as in a metropolis. There were dwellings of most every size and complexity, even high upon the side of the mountains. Here and there similar *carialds* stood erect, pointing towards the blue sky. And each contour was strangely familiar to him. All covered, as if by a sprawling mantle of twinkling, busy light set fast upon the wide sweep of topography like a distant city at summer daybreak. They reached the peculiar man who was standing in a circle of gentle light which sprang from the ground bathing him in a sheath of calm. At its perimeter were arrayed a display of flowers of every colour and composition, the like of which he had never seen before.

The man looked down, his brown, sunny skin clean shaven, straight black ribbons of hair hung to his broad chest from either side of a long face which was both stern and proud. Yet under a great hook nose, his mouth began a kindly smile. Jonathan felt the lady's touch slip from his and her slim hands lifted toward the glittering helm. She took the brightest gemstone from the array and together, hand upon hand, they pressed it tenderly to boy's forehead. As Jonathan was drawn back across the beautiful green hillside, he recognised his familiarity, but it was now certainty. These were the lands about Hendre Bach farm. The dotted cottages, lines of unbroken stone walls, forests, roads and harsh standing stones were no longer there. Only the elemental root and bone of the ancient land itself remained. What Jonathan saw was as real as everyday before it vanished like a soft gentle breeze, but with a potency as enormous as the earth Herself. With it passed his consciousness for a short time. Then from nowhere he rallied, moving across a time-filled chasm with Deldramena holding his hand again to see a huge motorcar swing around a great city square. It stopped behind another limousine at the end of a glittering queue. He saw a handsome man in the back of the chauffeur driven motorcar. And there, sitting alongside was his mother. The man had his arm about her.

'You and I, Siân, will be following a route which could not be bettered by the King and Queen of England...' The words rang out, clear, bold.

Fast alert now, Jonathan watched them in awe. The queue moved slowly forward. An immaculately uniformed courtesan was opening shining motorcar doors one by one, allowing well-dressed party-goers to emerge at the floodlit entrance of a palace, Jonathan heard a lady say that this was the fascist showcase to the world.

The car in front of his mother's limousine had discharged its grand occupants and she was looking up at the respectfully smiling face of the official as he opened her car door. She emerged into brilliant light before the stately entrance, long fluted stone columns rose either side to a pediment of Grecian styled splendour. But all Jonathan could understand was that his mother should not be there at all.

Inside the entrance, guests were walking through a huge passageway to what looked like formal gardens further on. His mother's handsome escort was suddenly at her side. Two blackshirted *squadrista* flanking the entrance, badges and regalia about them, stepped forward when they saw the big impressive man. Each gave a smart fascist salute.

Siân thrilled at the action and looked about to see discretely stationed *carabiniere* standing fully armed and alert as her companion showed his Party identification. And it was very clear to the frightened boy that his mother was so enraptured. He had not thought to look down at himself until now and saw bare feet and his threadbare pyjama trousers. No one took any notice.

The buzz of voices inside the passage was electric and soon the man, now seen and respected as a high ranking member of Benito Mussolini's Brotherhood of Fascists, a beautiful woman at his side, stood by opened black wrought iron gates before the inner courtyard.

'God, this is all wonderful, David...'

Jonathan was on tip toe; a finger touch away from his mother's lovely face. He had lost all fear in an inkling of rage. He moved so near to the big blond man that he could see clever steel blue eyes sparkling in the light of bright electric lamps high above them, ardour written clear. The man moved very close to her and Jonathan wanted to push him away.

'Did I not promise that you would be here to experience all this with me?'

She smiled beautifully, took his arm and they walked forward, rubbing shoulders with the powerful, elegant, rich and famous of the world.

Now at will, without effort, ten-year-old Jonathan Webster could not only see and hear any conversation he chose from the vast gathering, but also the dark silhouette of his tiny bedroom far away at Hendre Bach farm - even William asleep in the next bed. And there was no need to be afraid, Deldramena had told him so.

After what seemed only a few moments, attention was taken by the sound of ringing bells. An announcement was made that a banquet would be commencing in thirty minutes and would the Duce's honoured guests like to make their way up the stairs to the great hall, *Sala Regia*, in preparation.

They returned to the building through the gates and climbed the huge marble stairwell to the first floor. Siân was completely enthralled by the wonder about her. In all past travels; London, Paris, Berlin and other European cities, she had never seen anything quite so august as this. And to her young son it was so obviously, painfully clear that she was smitten. He began to cry. The room's enormous size dwarfed everything, including the huge embellished doors at each end. Three great rings hung from the ceiling; heavy, vigorously carved and sparkling with many electric lights. Row after row of exquisitely laid out tables ran across the room from windows set one above the other and everywhere there was bustle and grandeur. Women in the most delightful evening dresses - Chanel, Lanvin and Molyneux haute couture - were almost commonplace. Men handsome and proud talked, gesticulated and laughed, many in evening clothes, others in tailored military uniforms with black shirts, fascist badges and regalia. David Templeman took the arm of the beautiful Lady Siân Webster to his own, adoration evident still in his face, then he escorted her graciously out into the heart of the great banqueting hall, to merge quickly among Italy's fascist elite.

Many heads turned when Italy's undisputed dictator strode out into his banquet like a Roman Caesar - just as he intended. He wore an immaculate grey serge army dress uniform, blue stripes ran down the sides of his bulging trousers which were tucked into black, highly polished jack-boots. Little Welsh Siân Williams peeked out from behind the grand lady she had become, watching spell-bound as Benito Mussolini merged among groups of honoured guests to move on through to Blackshirts and notables, whilst she was forced to offer practised small talk still, rather than stare as she wanted at this fascist colossus.

Templeman was tall, and to Jonathan stunning still, both in appearance and conduct. His beguiling charm remained unmatched. The boy, an unseen shadow at his side, only knew he hated this man now more than anything or anyone he had ever hated in his life. The couple circulated easily, shadowed by their silent escort, ending up with a group of high-ranking *gerachi* and their wives. As they moved on again, Jonathan tried to stand between them, but could not. Templeman indicated discretely. Lady Webster turned to see Mussolini striding towards his ministers whilst flunkies scurried speedily out of his path. The great banquet hall fell to silence as the *Duce* took his place on a throne-like chair at the head of a huge U-shaped table at the far end, and twenty-eight of his black-shirted, Grand Council ministers stood stiffly to give him the fascist salute.

One lifted his voice across the magnificent room as he had been ordered. 'Ladies and gentlemen, please ask the attendants for your places and be seated for the *Duce's* banquet.'

Jonathan was fast awake as William poured ice cold water into a cracked bowl and started to wash soon after five a.m. The older boy turned, rubbing his dark face with a ragged towel and saw Jonathan staring at him, the new light from the little window lighting his eyes.

'You're awake early.'

'William. I saw my mother last night. She was at a great party in Rome...'

The Welsh lad pulled on his shirt. 'Just a dream lad.' Then his short trousers. 'That's all.' Then his socks and shoes. 'Get a move on.'

Jonathan said nothing. He felt word foolish but nothing more. Soon he was washed and dressed, using the water from the cracked bowl after William. The jug was quite heavy by itself to carry up and down each day so whoever was up first got the clean water to wash in. He lifted the jug and followed William down the steep little stair to wake up calls from Nain Hendre.

The following night Deldramena took him again, as gentle as starlight.

Over 3,000 miles beyond Hendre Bach, in a backwater among the farming fields of Indiana, James Webster stood by his bed, unaware of Deldramena's ethereal presence as he searched in vain for the first faint glimmer of dawn through a dusty attic window. Tiredness and worry lines were clearly visible in the moonlight. An owl hooted and through the little window, a million cold stars filled their consciousness.

Slowly, instinct whispered Jonathan to be safe and well. It was a gentle feeling but so strong that he had no doubts at all. He had done all he could. Eleanor was sensible enough and the boy would be fine. But why had Siân left so suddenly without warning? She didn't want a failed businessman. A bankrupt. That was for certain. Never mind the world slump, he was finished in England, perhaps for good. Jonathan saw only his father's pain, nothing more and let go of Deldramena's hand to reach out, but there was a chasm there as wide as the world. He heard the hooting owl now and watched as its eerie call pulled him away.

Just over a week later Nain called him after the family had eaten breakfast. He had told no one about Deldramena and seeing his Mum and Dad in a dream. Not a word. Gwen was washing up the dishes when she called him over.

'Are you still finding it hard working in the vegetable garden, Jon Bach?'

The boy nodded and picked up a tea towel such his improved domesticity.

She smiled the kindly Nain smile he looked for, giving approval. 'I think you are doing better than you think. Would you like a break this morning and run an errand for me up to Nainy Hafod?'

Jon nodded. 'It's rather a long way though.'

'Nonsense'. She lifted a big black pan. 'Big boy like you should be back in no time.' Gwen cocked a mischievous eye. 'Afterwards I want you back in that garden weeding all the way down to Princes's stable and no messing.'

'Oh, Nain. My hands are sore and my knees too…'

Ten minutes later Jonathan was walking urgently past white-washed farm buildings, along the small path by the pig sty and out into Cae Bach. In the wicker basket he carried was laid a pile of newly picked St. John's Wort, carefully cut willow bark and some odd plants he had never seen before. In his pocket folded neatly was a note in Gwen's gentle hand for her mother. It was a nice, fresh day, clouds scudding across Moel Seisiog didn't bode ill weather and the sun was coming out shining brightly. Soon he was over the gate at the back of the farmhouse and climbing manfully the steeply rising hendre pastures, the long haul of hafod lifting away steeply ahead. He leapt the bubbling stream – where he and William had watched Tomos the hare darting away from their nosiness - and after ten minutes sat down to rest and stare about. The wind had got up. It was warm, but enough to cool a sweating little body. He looked hard towards Snowdon and down towards the Conwy valley far below him. What a wonderful place this is to live, if only he could become as tough as William, Taid and Nain and the family. He wondered if he ever could. His knee was hurting from a ragged cut where he fell in the vegetable garden. He had washed it with water from the watering can and it had stopped bleeding in a few minutes. He told no one of this – a habit now – so the family couldn't call him soft or daft.

Then the English townee was up and cresting the hill. Jon Bach ran pell mell taking a precarious path among large rocks and stands of prickly gorse without a stop. He turned at the high cliff seen from the top of the hafod and now took a winding route towards Nain and Taid Hafod's strange, big bouldered cottage. He entered the boundary made up of standing slates, ran down the path of beaten earth and stones right up to the black oak door without stopping. Slowly the wicker basket was lowered to the ground and even more slowly he sat down on the slate step. Chasing with William for weeks had toughened Jonathan, but not so much that it would allow Nainy Hafod to see him gasping for air. He checked that Nain's note was safe in his pocket and just as he was regaining himself he heard the iron latch lift quietly and turned with the creak of the heavy old door.

Wide eyes looked up as Nainy Hafod peered out from the gloom for the sun was bright overhead now.

'Jon Bach!' Her clear, husky voice fell to Welsh and then she changed to English in an instant. 'Come in, Jon and welcome. Are you thirsty? What have you got there for me, cariad? Weeds from your new Nainy? No William, where is he, boy? Have you run all the way without him?'

Jonathan was taken by surprise at the torrent of questions and then more came quickly, one on top of the other as he was ferried happily past the little stove with its cheery open doors and on into Nain and Taid Hafod's parlour, where she bade him sit on an ancient polished country chair whilst she settled at a little oak table to pour them both a drink of root beer. He slurped down much of the contents without a stop, took out the note from Gwen and began a careful reply to all her questions as politely as he could. As he did so, Jonathan found himself staring at the kindly face so intent upon him, a mass of white hair tied back with a ribbon looked white as snow. Her face was brown, weathered and much wrinkled with a lovely little turned up button nose. Blue eyes, sharp as twinkles from the little stream on the hendre far below were taking all of him in carefully, for this was the first time they had been together without other distractions.

She was amazed to see how very much like Siân, her estranged granddaughter he was. It made a joyous shiver run as she hung on every English word. The predilection was returned equally, for he saw a kindness in her old face which was as open as it was strong. Jon Bach felt at ease immediately. He looked out through the diamond window pane to the sweep of the hills and, having answered all Nainy Hafod's questions carefully and politely which she noted with pride and pleasure, began to ask some of his own. It would set in motion talk about a dark subject that the old lady would never have guessed could come from anyone other than folk of true Celtic blood.

'William says you're a doctor with weeds – herbs. You help the family and people who are ill.'

The old lady nodded. 'That is so.'

'Then are you a witch, Nainy?'

Morfydd's old eyes smiled gently, as if the boy had asked for more root beer. 'No. Not in the sense you mean, Jon Bach. But my old Nain,' she acknowledged his lack of Welsh, 'grandmother as you would say, taught me much of the lore of this old land and I have learned much more since I was a young girl.'

Suddenly hope opened in Jonathan's heart. He felt he could trust this old Welsh lady – his blood great grandmother – as no one else. He decided to tell her about Deldramena. Her visits to him at night when

73

asleep and how she would take him to see his mother and father. She alone would not think him mad.

Jonathan's words had the simple honesty ten years and some brings. No guile. No hedging. No self evaluation. Morfydd's eyes remained clear and firm, a little damp perhaps, her wise countenance gentle still as her Jon Bach told the truth of what he remembered on those special nights and how he had woken in the morning feeling bright, as if he had slept without disturbance, and how William had not believed him once and how he had kept his own counsel after that.

Wisdom is a fragile, ethereal human building block to one's make up, put together from experience, emotions and judgement. Then enhanced by the chance of location – and for Nainy Hafod this mix from life, plus her Welsh ancestry had given an astuteness for the world around her that was quite remarkable.

'I have heard that name only once before.'

Jon stared across the little table. 'You believe me, Nainy?'

She made no reply for a while and then pointed out of the window. 'There was an Englishman who lived down at Capel Garmon years ago now. He loved this land, speaking Welsh to us all but with an obvious English accent, making no attempt to be anything other than what he was - an Englishman who loved these hills and valleys, our rivers and forests and was content to be left alone.' She laughed sweetly. 'Harry Davis came from a town called, Reading in Berkshire, I expect you've heard of it, Jon Bach?'

He nodded and finished his glass which was refilled.

'Everyone liked Harry Davis for he learned of our ways, tiling the soil, fencing, forestry work. He could split slate as well as any Welshman at the quarry and was a good shepherd too. Yet he remained aloof from folk, not better, just...' she paused '...English. As if away from home, on holiday. Because of this he kept himself to himself and made only one real friend, Taid Hafod, your great grandfather and my dear husband. They liked to sit and watch the world go by with pipes of good tobacco and frothy heads to their pints of beer down at the White Hart in Capel Garmon.

Jonathan was still only ten years old. His newly acquired great grandmother realised that her talk was as much for herself in reminiscing, as for the boy and she finished quickly. 'Poor Harry is dead now, but he spoke to me of Deldramena once when we met.'

Jon Bach sat up with a start, the root beer slopping. 'Really, Nainy. Really?'

She nodded gently. He talked of a beautiful lady who led him back to England where he saw his wife and a brother."

I too have had similar experiences over my long life. The lady was not called Deldramena when she came to me. I cannot recall a name. Many Welsh folk, if they are honest will talk of such things but most are stitched up, for fear of being thought foolish.

'We Celtic peoples are very, very old as a race. Your blood has been mingled with ours, Jon Bach. And yours is from a very old race too. The Saxon people. Do you know about the Saxons?'

'Dad told me that we were descended from a long line of English aristocracy going back to before Richard the Lionheart, King of England.'

'Perhaps this mingling has given you special insight.'

'What's insight?'

'The gift to see Deldramena and go with her so she can help you. This is a very old world, my little grandson.' Nainy Hafod sat back in her chair and sighed. 'I only know that you are gifted. Perhaps one day you will become a great man. But until then, learn to treasure this gift, learn how to use it well.

'When I was young, a wise person told me that Wales is much older than ever we could imagine. You gave a description of a circle of glittering pieces of crystal and the hills and mountains all around. Yet you knew it to be these very lands all about us. That picture in your head may have been from times long, long ago before our history books were even thought of. Or it could be a scene in the future that you entered and became part of. What is sure, Jon Bach, is that you must follow your gift and use it wisely. I also think you must have fallen in love with this great land of Wales for Deldramena to have taken you as she did. Remember how Harry Davis, who was proud to be English like you, loved Wales very much and was also visited by a lady he called Deldramena.'

Jonathan Webster felt a warm glow inside him now. Nainy Hafod was the best great grandmother he could ever have wished for. Soon Taid Hafod arrived home, tired but happy. He had been down to Llanrwst on a friend's horse and cart for supplies, had had a good few ales in two pubs and had met some old friends. Both Morfydd and Elias showed their new great grandson around their humble little smallholding and soon, with much love, they let Jon be on his way back down the meadows to Hendre Bach cottage where the family were in need of him. Jonathan left with a stronger spring in his step and the realisation in his young heart that life in the hills might not be as bad as he had first thought.

## Nine

### Seven Weeks Later

To the south west, at the foot of Pen y Rhiwlas, curling lines of smoke rose in the early light of day as if pulled by invisible hands from the cottage chimneys of Capel Garmon village, whilst Welsh mothers inside were bustling about their kitchens making early cups of tea and breakfasts. At the top of Pen y Rhiwlas, Jonathan Webster looked down the great steep incline of sweet highland grasses and ancient stone walls to Uncle Ianto's farm at the northern end of the village, then out across the beautiful Conwy valley to Moel Siabod. From its great skirts, a long sweep of wonderful panorama could be seen rising away into the distance; Yr Wyddfa - the peak of Snowdon and Crib Goch were just visible next to Siabod, then standing out clearly against a brightening sky, the Glyders, Tryfan, Carnedd Dafydd, Carnedd Llewelyn and Foel Fras far off to the right.

There was still a tang of dawn in the air and the smell of sweet woodland scents which had been lifted by a light rain the night before orchestrated the senses. Between the peaks of Siabod and Foel Fras, the undulating deep greens and browns of Gwydyr Forest lay at the feet of Snowdon's beautiful Ladies in a sombre, basking silence. To the left, the little town of Betws-y-Coed was hidden beyond a fold in the hillside and then away in the distance, unseen from even the boy's majestic vantage point were the villages and towns of Dolwyddelan, Blaenau Ffestiniog and Beddgelert. All in all, a mighty scene.

The aristocrat's son turned to William who was peeing against a wall. The Welsh boy shook himself and pulled the leg of his short trousers down. 'We've got four hours at the most before Taid wants us up on the high moorlands to lift some more peat with him. I had to promise we'd be back in time so we could stay the night at Uncle Ianto's. It's taken weeks and weeks to get him to let us go. Now, do you want to see Old Silas' secret place?'

'What is it? You won't tell me.'

William gave a frustrated, superior look. 'Well if you must know, it's a Roman Temple in a cave.' He glared, dark eyes angry. 'Well do you?'

'Do I?' The freckled face lit up. 'Boy that's what I've been waiting for ever since I got here! Wow a secret cave .......!'

'We've got just enough time if we hurry.' You'll need to run fast though, ifn we're going to get back in time.'

'How far?'

'Well from here I reckon it's well over a mile to Squire's Wood and then,' he paused, 'say two miles to the cave.' The farm boy grinned. Come, Jon Bach. Let's see you really run!'

They set off across the high flanks of Pen y Rhiwlas at a testing pace and picked a varied path across sheep meadows, through stands of bracken and whin, about gullies and on through sparse patches of trees stunted by wind and weather, gradually dropping down from the higher ground towards a tiny ribbon of road which worked itself along from the village, past fields and dark woods to the A5 London to Holyhead road. William could run. His English cousin, who had lost most of his suburban softness now, was a sterling companion and made the very best of every undertaking William drew him into after their long days of hard but happy labour on Hendre farm.

Jonathan ran safe, strong steps either behind his young mentor or alongside him, and as the boys covered furlong after furlong of testing, rugged Welsh countryside, he thought of the warnings about being caught in Squire's wood; of the stories William had told him, even a few days after he and Aunt Eleanor had arrived at the farm and how the boys had followed the ancient stream called Afon Gallt-y-Gwg to the very edge of Squire's land. Jonathan remembered sitting on the long, easy branch of the old alder tree which reached out over the meandering stream, a place where elves and strange creatures were supposed to lurk - named, so the legend said, to commemorate the terrible massacre of a cohort of Roman Legionaries by the Celtic Leader Lenathay, who had fired the hill in high summer. The English boy was filled with the wonder of it all and by the challenge. It felt like ice was in the sweat of his nimble exertions as they ran on and on down the wild, free pasture slopes like young Grecian athletes of old. Soon they had passed Gwninger farm higher up on the hillside and cut a sharp path down towards the Capel Garmon road. The two runners crossed the twisting lane by Pentre-bach farm and worked their way over fields with ragged dry stone walls tumbling the slopes. The great wood above them crept nearer and before long, at about hundred yards from its first sentinel trees, they stopped to catch breath and laid themselves out on a carpet of sweet mountain grasses strewn with cascades of wild Welsh poppies.

Where's the river?'

'River?'

'Afon Gallt-y-Gwg,' Jonathan stumbled the words, 'the one we followed to the edge of Squire's wood and you said meant angry something and was named after all the Roman soldiers who died.'

'Yes. River of the Angry Hill, as is said in English. Look up there.' William pointed across the vale to a high dark line of woodlands crowning the top of a long hill, his dark eyes aflame. 'She twists her path through the weald up there,' he turned, 'that's where we saw the family of otters playing in the pool, you remember? It's a mystical place, Jon Bach, and no mistake. Afterwards she runs on for miles to skirt the far end of Squire's wood before entering the River Conwy. C'mon.' William jumped to his feet and sprinted away up the hillside, making a direct challenge of physical prowess in everything but word and his English cousin followed immediately.

They ran on, side by side in an affinity of panting silence, neither giving way or slowing the fast pace one jot. As the high timberland grew near William seemed to increase the pace until they passed its outlying oaks, then a dark green cloak cast a sudden embrace of heart-wood, fauna and guarding silences about them. Jonathan stared around excitedly as he continued after his friend. The enchantment of the thicket was burnished by radiant sun-shafts striking beams of golden light through high canopies of beech, elm, sycamore and oak. Tamarisk and wild strawberries grew here in profusion, toadstools, puffballs and clamouring tendrils of creeper plants interspersed among the tree roots were writhing slow, determined paths out of a verdant flower carpeted floor.

'C'mon, Jon Bach, you're falling behind!'

'Never. You can't lose me.'

They leapt across long forgotten stone walls now little more than shallow lines of sphagnum and lichen, shrouding forgotten plans of long dead gentry, or old Celtic demarcation lines cut by ancient men into the good earth even before those misty times of master and peasant had made their indelible mark upon the face of Wales. Over rotting trunks of great trees they romped and scurried, on through small sunny green glades with boundaries of tall gorse and bracken in which few men now ever trod, where nature ruled unchallenged; they fought for playful dominance, hoping to see the other boy slow, but neither could get the upper hand. All the time William insisted on silence and both made little more than a rustle as they passed across gulley, leapt rivulet stream or slippery grass slope, for the wily son-o'-the-land knew only too well of Mr. Kenton, Squire Bellamy's evil-minded new gamekeeper, most of it from first hand experience.

Suddenly, William raised his arm and they both stopped dead. The wooded land ahead was starting to fall steeply now towards the floor of the Conwy valley, still unseen through the blanket of trees. A twelve foot wide gulley had been cut into the hillside a few feet ahead by the action of ice-age glaciers, it looked like a narrow man-made road, save for persistent slim trees growing here and there on its stony floor. Such was its aspect among the rugged terrain that a wayward or lost traveller of old would have thought its leafy route down a godsend. They both stared at the ancient track in silence for a few moments, regaining their breath.

'This is where the doomed cohort of the Twentieth Roman Legion marched and were ambushed by King Lenathay.' William's words were whispered and he indicated for his friend to remain very quiet. 'Squire's gamekeeper patrols up and down here regularly, you'll see why in a moment.'

They stepped cautiously into the defile and strode down for about two hundred yards to where a buttress of mica imbedded granite rock stood like an ancient sentry station among a stand of quickbeam trees. The track bent a narrow line around the huge glistening rock and then opened out again. There, the natural way changed to a less friendly, yet still quite accessible path. Travellers over thousands of years had walked out from this natural gulley to continue down, treading a dirt road to the valley floor, still quite some distance below them.

William pointed. 'You see that long dip in the ground running across this course? That's where Celtic warriors dug their deep trench down the hillside and set sharpened stakes in the bottom of it to bar the path of the Roman legionaries who were fleeing the fires their comrades had set. Come on!'

They walked a short distance through the trees, both boys keeping their eyes open for any sign of Kenton, but they came across no living thing save the sound of birds and a rabbit which rushed across their silent path. The boys stopped at the trench. Time had almost filled it in, but the effort of the Celtic soldiers nearly 1600 years before had not fully obliterated what had been done in the name of warfare and man's timeless inhumanity to man.

'Uncle Emyr found this spot. It is where the battle was finally won. He said that down there in the gulley are the remains of many Roman soldiers. He used to dig down in this place years ago when Squire weren't so cranky and he found bits of things including a leg bone.'

'Your Uncle Emyr's dead now?'

William nodded, his darkling curls bouncing. 'It was whilst he was exploring around here that he found the entrance to the temple. Look!'

Jonathan turned and followed the Welsh boy's outstretched arm. A split in the side of the buttress rock was almost unnoticeable hidden among plant growth, for it was little more than the shoulder width of a big man. William led the way through and it opened out after about twenty-five feet into a steep-sided rocky enclosure; up above the blue sky glowed through overhanging trees. To the right stood an ancient white marble portico built against the sheer rock wall consisting of two weathered fluted pillars with a roofed pediment above. Under it, an ancient black studded oak door on great iron hinges guarded the entrance.

William turned and looked at his cousin's astonished face. Uncle Emyr first brought me here secretly when I was eight years of age - although I'd been here before on my own. He said that this porch was not built by the Romans. Even in this hidden spot it would have weathered much more because of rain running down the cliff-face. He reckoned Squire Bellamy's ancestors built it about 300 years ago. The Bellamy family have owned this land for at least 400 years and Uncle Emyr said they must have known about the temple for a long time but kept it secret; a sort of mysterious family tradition they were sworn to keep from the world, handing it down from one generation to the next and it has finally made the present Squire go completely potty.'

Jonathan looked frightened.

'Don't worry. It's not haunted or anything, I've been here loads of times. It's lovely inside, we'll go in, you'll see. Poor old Squire Bellamy was a soldier in the Great War, like my Dad, except being gentry, he was an officer. They didn't know until afterwards of course, but those battles had started to turn his mind. Now he's mad as a March hare. He goes about these woods anytime night or day dressed up in a red tail-coat and riding on a big white horse like a lord from years gone by. It's then that he becomes Old Silas. They say there is a great painting of a family ancestor in the banqueting room at the manor house which was painted before the time of Napoleon. Squire has the man's old-fashioned clothes exactly, down to the last detail, including a blunderbuss gun and a ball-shot pistol. Evan Jones Milk at school told me, his elder sister, Carys used to work at manor house for a spell, she's seen him dressed up and the great painting on the wall as well. When Squire's wearing the old fashioned clothes he guards this temple and these woods with his life. They say if a man challenged him then, he would die before yielding. Silas is that mad. That's why some folks around here have named him, Old *Mad* Silas. Mr Kenton, the gamekeeper is employed by Squire's wife for a lot of money so that he will keep his mouth shut about all these funny goings on. Poor devil. They'd take Squire away to Denbigh if it got out.'

Jonathan had lost his fear now, such was the tale. 'Denbigh?'

'The asylum's at Denbigh. But the funny thing is, at Church on Sunday morn, Squire reads the lesson, good as gold - you'd never know he was mad, never guess it in a thousand years. And if he passes you in his carriage or the new motorcar, he'll nod his ol' head and smile just like any real Squire should. Poor man.' William put his hand on his hips. 'Just goes to show. He comes here a lot you know. Cefyn Davies from yonder Pentre farm who poaches about these hills, says he's seen Old Silas head this way on moonlit nights, especially full moon. It seems this old Roman temple was the last straw that has finally turned Squire's mind. Perhaps a family secret is too much to keep when it's lasted for 400 years.'

William turned a ring handle and pushed the heavy door part way open. It was pitch black inside the cave-temple. He picked up a stubby candle set in a silver candleholder from a little table just visible in the gloom beyond the door and passed it out to Jonathan. 'Hold that.' He returned, fumbled out a box of matches from the darkness and gave them to Jonathan standing under the portico. 'Here, light the candle whilst I see if Mr Kenton's about.'

Jonathan put the candle down on the marble floor, took out a match as he was bid and made an attempt at lighting it, whilst William worked his way back down the narrow passage between the rock faces to the path outside. He came back in a short while, the candle flickering into life.

William looked at his young cousin, Celtic eyes sparkling a strange, knowing look which lit his face beyond twelve boyhood years. 'Mithras was a Persian god who the Roman army adopted. Uncle Emyr told me all about it. Jesus Christ and Mithras were right alongside each other as Roman religions at one time, Christianity standing for loving kindness and non-aggression, Mithraism for stern military virtues. They were bound to fall out sooner or later. And they did. The celebration of the birth of Mithras is December the twenty-fifth, Christmas day, Jesus' birthday. Their temples were much like Christian temples in layout and they used bread, water and wine in ritual, just like the Christians. But it was the Christians who persecuted the Mithraists, not the other way around, smashing their altars and wrecking their holy places, even though Christians were supposed to be non-violent - you know, turn the other cheek and all that stuff. They made sure that every temple to Mithras was smashed to pieces because it was so near to their own ideas for worship and in all of Britain, this must be the only one to have survived. That's what Uncle Emyr said! I told you it was built in memory of the cohort that was slain by King Lenathay. My uncle said this must have been one of the last they ever built.'

The silence was ornamented by two Red Admiral butterflies which had worked a way along the rock gap and now double-danced above the boys' heads.

William pushed the door and lifted the flickering candle high. 'C'mon. See for yourself.'

They crossed the threshold side by side, feeling a sudden change to cold, their eyes which had been focused in the bright daylight were now temporarily blinded by the cave's near pitch blackness. Jonathan watched the candle flame and quite quickly he made out four pairs of fluted pillars leading ahead. On each was a bronze cone-shaped lamp, William touched his candle to the lamps as they walked into the temple, the increased light revealing a beautiful mosaic tiled floor beneath their feet about eight foot wide running between the pillars. Suddenly Jonathan grabbed the Welsh boy's shoulder and pointed ahead. There on a stone table, was the outline of a man's head with a peculiar halo of light behind it.

'What's that, William?' There was near terror in his whispered voice.

Spooky, isn't it? There's a little bit of light coming through a split in the wall behind his head, that's all. It was done on purpose. When you come in and your eyes get accustomed to the darkness, the first thing you see is the Mithras head glowing! The Mithraists, cut a shelf in the rock right before the hole and put a slab of marble on top for their high altar table. It's like a Christian walking up to the cross of Jesus and it shining in the dark for no reason.'

William continued lighting the lamps until they stood before the altar. The god's face didn't look very scary, almost kind Jonathan thought, a bit like a lady with curly long hair and a strange cap at the back of her head. The boys turned and looked about them in the now adequate light of eight lamps. The roof remained unworked, a large vault with mineral reflections glinting here and there, but the walls had been built up to a height of ten feet or more with precisely cut stone blocks, so the temple took on a symmetrical rectangular shape. Similar blocks, but in various sizes, had been used to fashion three rows of benches which filled the space between the walls and the pillars on either side of the aisle, something like those running down the amphitheatre of Ancient Rome. Jonathan guessed that this was where the worshippers sat.

The block walls had alcoves set in them above the benches. In each, was a statue of ravens, bulls and lions. The Welsh boy led his friend along the highest bench and held up the candle so each sub-deity or symbol of the religion could be seen clearly. The statues were beautifully made out of clay and had been fired with coloured pigments to give a wonderful effect. Jonathan could hardly believe that each one was over 1500 years old.

'Uncle Emyr told me that being reasonably dry in here, with almost no daylight,' he pointed to the hidden fissure by the altar, 'the gentle breaths of air which come in every now and then from the altar and some through the doorway, have helped to keep all these things in nearly perfect condition.'

'Why does Squire Bellamy come here?'

'To worship Mithras.'

'Really?'

'Oh yes. I was caught here once.'

Jonathan's eyes widened.

'Had to hide behind that pillar.' He pointed. 'Old Silas came in, but he only lit two lamps by the high altar. I heard everything he said.'

What did he say?'

'Lots of words in a strange language - I think it was Latin.'

'Wow, William! Can you speak Latin? I have to do Latin at school. I hate it.'

The boy grinned proudly in the candlelight. 'No. I heard it spoken at a Catholic Church in Llandudno, the week before. We went by train to a wedding of a cousin on my mam's side. Anyway, I had to wait for nearly an hour in here before Squire finished and I could get out. He was praying to Mithras all right.'

'Why Mithras. Doesn't he like Jesus? Do you know?'

'I think it's because Squire was in the army in the Great War and the battles turned his mind, like I told you. Mithras is supposed to help all soldiers who ask of his help, no matter what.' The Welsh lad gave him a strange look. 'It was odd, you know, as if that old bust of Mithras was talking back to him and he could hear it, I'm sure he could, but it still looked like a lump of marble to me.'

The younger boy shivered, almost lost for words for the first time and looked about himself, finding the whole thing eerie and difficult now.

'Were you scared?'

'Wouldn't you have been?'

Jon nodded.

'Well then, there you are!'

Soon the two were putting out the lamps as time was short. William pulled the door shut behind him, they squinted into the daylight again and he kicked a stone casually. 'Did you like it, Jon Bach?'

His cousin nodded. They walked single file down the narrow path between the rock faces in solemn mood, stepping out onto the wood path, where a loud cry of glee rang out.

'Stand exactly where you are!' Malcolm Kenton strode away from the trees holding a very large twelve bore shotgun. He was dressed in a brown Norfolk shooting jacket, brown breeches with stout walking shoes and a check countryman's cap.

'Run!' William's cry had hardly left his mouth when the younger boy took to his heels and they ran neck and neck down the path.

No more than a couple of seconds later the man's loud, deep voice boomed out again. 'Halt or I'll shoot!'

William pulled Jonathan back by his arm and they turned to see Mr Kenton striding slowly towards them, the big gun raised up to his shoulder and a beady eye set along the double barrels.

'Gotcha! I've been after you for ages, young fella.' His eyes switched to Jonathan. 'But you're new to me. What's your name?'

'Say nothing, Tom bach.'

Jonathan looked at William.

'Oh, so it's Tom is it?'

The two boys stared at each other for a moment, Jonathan realising the other's quick guile.

'Get back in there where you've just come from - now!' He indicated with the gun towards the opening in the high rock face and then marched them back into it angrily, sticking the gun barrels in William's back and pushing him roughly until they were out of the cleft and before the temple threshold. The Welsh lad took it without a murmur.

'Open the door. Go on, you've both been in there, haven't you?'

William did as he was told. Kenton smiled. It was a long thin smile like someone about to eat a meal he had been relishing for a long while. Jonathan felt terrified but couldn't take his eyes off the weather-beaten face. There was something strange about the man's voice, his big ginger handlebar moustache and insolent manner, it seemed all the more mysterious somehow because he was a gamekeeper. His clothes were gentry clothes too, not a working man's and his voice...

Move back and let me in the doorway.' Kenton put his hand up above the little table where they had returned the candle and pulled out the end of a long rope. He stared triumphantly at William. 'You may be a clever young whippersnapper, but you didn't know about this, did you? Come here.' He handed the rope to the Welsh boy. 'On the other end of this rope is a bell. I found a rotting bell tower up on the top of this crag last April. It's over a narrow hole which goes all the way down into the beginning of the cave. I've mended the bell-pivot and put a new rope on the wheel.'

As the smile turned into a leer, Jonathan realised that the man had a Birmingham accent - at least he sounded very much like their rich next door neighbour back in Croydon who had moved down from Birmingham. So why would a well-off man from Birmingham be working as a gamekeeper miles from civilisation in North Wales?

Malcolm Kenton's leer made him look marginally more unpleasant than normal. 'I know what you little hill Welshies call Mr Bellamy,' the stocky man paused, weighing his words, '...when he is out on his rounds. You call him Old Silas, don't you?'

The boys could see the gamekeeper's face sweating now.

'Old Mad Silas, some say. Yes I know alright, I've got my spies. Well Old Silas is out on his rounds right now. And he knows that a few clangs from that old bell up there means, come quick, there's something wrong!' He let out a loud, spiteful laugh and lifted the gun towards William. 'Go on you horrible little pauper, ring for Old Mad Silas now, he wants a word with you two and he'll come at a gallop when you call...'

The boy remained still, his face unemotional. The gamekeeper walked across and stuck the gun hard into his ribs and snarled. 'Ring it, damn you to hell!'

'Go on, William, before he shoots!'

'William is it?' Kenton turned his head quickly. 'Well, well.'

'Sorry, I didn't think.'

The trapped farm boy could see his cousin was near to panic and tried to calm him, but before his words were finished, Kenton's voice rasped out harshly, drowning him out. 'Ring that damned bell! Ring the bell! Ring the bell! Ring the bell!' He lifted the gun menacingly, eyes like a wild animal's and the rope slowly started to stir. Jonathan was staring at his friend madly now, but he could do nothing. Faster the rope moved, harder tugs each time as if it had a life of its own and William was merely an anchor point at one end. The boy's strong wiry arms were nearly at full stretch when the first shock reverberations suddenly rang out and fell down the great stone bank like a waterfall. The deep knell rolled loudly across the wooded slopes beyond the constricted entrance of the mithraeum, demanding attention, spreading its clamour about woodlands far and wide.  If anyone was awaiting that warning knell, they couldn't miss it.

Jonathan Webster was small for his ten years and very scared. How he actually managed to summon the courage to make a dive at Malcolm Kenton's big twelve bore shotgun remained a mystery.  He wasn't stupid, just terrified perhaps of confronting this crazy man on a big white horse whilst trapped with his back to a rock wall.  The gamekeeper yelled out in sudden alarm as Jonathan grabbed the gun, immediately William let go of the rope, it vanished into the darkness and he leapt out of the temple doorway a split second after Kenton threw little Jonathan Webster across the stony walled enclosure like a toy.

'Run for it, Thomas, run as hard as you can!'  William's strong young hands were about the blued barrels now, man and boy wrestled for control.'

'Run, Thomas, run.'

Jonathan got to his feet quickly.  He wasn't hurt, but instead of running away, he grabbed Kenton around the neck whilst William continued to shout for him to go using the false name.  He needed to throw the wild gamekeeper off their scent by using any ruse and there wasn't much available.  Suddenly the gun came out of Malcolm Kenton's hands and he fell heavily to the ground.  Jonathan fell with him, but scrabbled clear and was up in a second to disappeared into the rock cleft whilst the elder boy threw the gun to the far side of the portico - about twenty feet away from the narrow passage - then he ran after his friend as fast as he could.  A quick glance showed Kenton to be winded but moving determinedly towards his gun.  When William emerged from the crevice, Jonathan had run straight across the path outside and was starting down the bank into the trees.

'Jonathan!  Not that way!'

The youngster stopped with a slither and looked back.  They both reacted as a muffled curse came from deep within the rock cleft, Mr Kenton was not very far away.

'You haven't time to climb back.  He'll be here in seconds.' William turned back, terror near his normally calm face.  He looked down the slope again.  'Get running, Jon Bach.  Fast as ever you can.'  He pointed to the right.  'Go that way, down to the main road by the Conwy river, then work your way over the fields and back up along the Nebo road to Hendre Bach farm.  I'll head him off this way.'  With that he shot off up the path like a hare.

Jonathan Webster nodded and waved as he scurried away into the brushwood and was gone from sight in seconds.  The Welsh boy had decided to run back up the steep path returning through the woods along the same route they had originally taken. He guessed Kenton would lose his breath quicker that way and Hendre Bach was in its general direction, perhaps less than an hour from the temple at a good run. He had to draw the gamekeeper away somehow, but still have the opportunity of getting back home first to warn the family if Jonathan failed to turn up. God. What would Nain and Taid say. It would all be his fault. William decided to start near the farm and work his way back down the long road towards Llanrwst first, before raising the alarm. With any luck they would meet up somewhere along it and things could yet turn out for the best.

*    *    *

Squire Charles Bellamy's big, pure white stallion blew through its nostrils and he felt the sweating animal lift its head sharply. He eased back on the reins and the beautiful horse stopped near the entrance to a small sun-dappled meadow in the ancient woodlands of Coed Cilcennus. Through the overhanging trees his sharp, nervous eyes picked out what the horse had already smelt, someone was walking straight towards him, quite oblivious of his presence through distraction and seemingly in a hurry. The rich land-owner touched the stallion's flanks gently and moved out into the bright sunlight with his blunderbuss gun pointing at the newcomer. 'Frenchie. Halt or I shoot!'

Jonathan Webster looked up into the huge flared barrel and then into the face of the strangest man on or off a horse he had ever seen in his life. The gun holder was dressed like an aristocrat from 150 years ago. Tricorne hat, a poppy red silk tail-coat with mother-of-pearl buttons, white breeches, burgundy waistcoat and old-fashioned buckled shoes. The tailcoat's sloping skirts, trimmed with blue, had narrow, blunted ends and were cast back across the horses flanks. White cotton stockings met his close fitting breeches beneath the knee and were held in place by a gold clasp, highly polished shoes with large silver buckles sat in silvered stirrups. The man thrust out his arm, white silk ruffles at the sleeve and pointed a wagging finger with a large diamond encrusted ring on it at the boy.

'Napoleon's spy, eh? Heard the bell tolling for you. Mr Kenton knows. He knows right enough and you're a French spy, me lad!'

'No, sir. I'm an English boy.' Jonathan's callow face stared up like an innocent, wide-eyed young animal.

88

Old Silas sat completely still, save for a hand which patted the horse's neck gently. Beneath the open red coat, a richly patterned brocade waistcoat with gold embroidery decoration had ebony buttons done up part way. A wide, white cravat in embroidered muslin bulged at his neck and folded doeskin gloves hung from a gold clasped strap attached to the tailcoat. William had warned him about the strange old-fashioned clothes, but he wasn't prepared for anything like this. Bellamy's face normally had a noble look to it, British aristocracy writ clear, but now, if time had suddenly faded backwards, he would be indistinguishable from the long dead lords and peacock fops of another age. Face-powder, rouge to his cheeks, a black velvet tricorne trimmed with a lace rosette and edged with gold braid sat well on the noble head; his powdered hair fastened low with a blue bow on the nape of his neck fell over the tail-coat's small silk collar.

'The deuce, you say.' He stared hard. 'English? Yer don't look it, boy. You look like a Frenchie to me. A child-spy for Napoleon.'

He moved closer, and rode the big white horse most skilfully around the motionless boy. 'English? Not Welsh?'

'Yes, sir.'

'You sound English. What's your name, boy?'

Jonathan's mouth formed around the name Thomas, but he thought better of the lie and spoke truthfully. 'Jonathan, sir.'

'What are you doing here on private land, Jonathan?'

'Looking for my friend.'

'Another boy?'

'Yes, sir. But he is not here.'

'How do you know?'

'I've looked.'

'You're alone?'

'Yes.'

'Are you an orphan then?'

'An orphan? No, sir - well my mother and father are away and I have no brothers or sisters.'

'So you are an orphan.'

'My father's gone to America, sir.'

'Ah. Is he a sailor?'

'Sort of, sir.'

'Sort of? Sort of? That's no good to me, boy.' The blunderbuss rose menacingly. 'What *sort of* is it to be? Be quick now, be quick, or Mr Kenton will have your tongue.'

'He's a captain, sir.' Suddenly Jonathan remembered the words from his father's letter which had arrived just two weeks before. He was to captain a great new aeroplane and maybe soon, would be back in England to take him home.

'A sea captain is it? Sailing the big Atlantic square-riggers, I'll be bound.'

Quite unexpectedly the blue blood looked more kindly at Jonathan. 'So you're a little orphan boy until he comes for you eh?'

'Yes, sir.'

The loud detonation of a shotgun suddenly lifted through the trees, echoing about for some moments and then carrion crows lifted from their hideaways, squawking coarse disapproval. Man and boy turned in the direction of the blast and after a few seconds the sound of Kenton's faint voice wafted across the dell, his threats of retribution should he get his hands on the young whippersnapper, quite unmistakable.

'Looks like Mr Kenton has found and lost your friend.' He looked down from the big white horse. 'When you catch up with him, tell him never to come here again. This is private land and people aren't welcome - except orphans.'

'Orphans, sir?'

'Poor orphans, maybe. If they're English and honest.

'Please, sir. Why are English orphans welcome and no one else?'

Old Silas took out a huge lace handkerchief from his silk breeches and wiped his nose. Rings with large precious stones set in gold glistened on delicate fingers. 'You're too inquisitive by far!'

He dug deep into his pocket and tossed a shiny silver coin down, which the boy caught easily. 'There's a shilling for you. Don't spend it all at once - in fact don't spend it at all! And don't lose it - ever. It'll bring you a hamper full o' good luck.'

'Thank you, sir.' Jonathan looked at the coin. It certainly wasn't a shilling - at least any shilling he had ever seen before.

Bellamy turned the stallion and straightened the tricorne, looking into the distance. 'It's enchanted, you see.' He looked back quickly. 'Understand? Magic. I might help orphans sometimes, if they're honest, mind. If you ever need help, little orphan boy and have no one else to turn to, you come and see Old Silas. I'm here most times, night or day. Butterscotch here knows these paths well enough and we often meander at night to search out Frenchies. You tell people that. He lifted the gun and shook it fiercely. We take no prisoners, you tell 'em that too from me, boy. Napoleon will never take these lands. If you really want my help, find the old bell and ring it. Understand?'

Jonathan nodded frantically, hardly believing his luck to be still living and hearing what he was hearing. Squire Bellamy's eyes seemed to glaze as if he was trying to recall some reality to mind, then he nipped at the horses powerful flanks, the silver buckled shoes glinted and he thundered down the meadow into the thicket, holding the gun high. A few seconds later Old Mad Silas had gone.

Jonathan looked down at his hand. The silver coin shone like brand new. He turned it over, inspecting both sides carefully. The name of King George III and the date 1787 stood out clearly and he drew in a sudden breath of astonishment.

The squire had roused himself somewhat like a drunk stirring from sleep, whilst I was playing out my role for the boy. 'Twas his worn, worldly body that I had inhabited, so I could hardy complain. Still, my life-force remained dominant over his - as ever. What stalwarts those boys are turning out to be. William has come a long way in my estimations, rising very agreeably when I moved through the wood and by that otter pool, yet he registered my presence well - as the animals always do of course. Now at last I had engaged Jonathan in wit and debate. She is right to want him guided. I will do all I can. The bare bones of childhood are there clearly to make a very special man. The time for testing will be coming soon enough.

# Ten

Jonathan knew the trouble he and William would be in if Nian and Taid found out about their escapade. As he wandered back though Coed Cilcennus, the sound of Buttercup's hooves and Old Silas' shouts of anger were still ringing in his ears. Jon set his mind on finding William fast so they could both get back to work on the hafod, cutting out peat with their grandfather. Taid and the hafod seemed a long way off as he broke into a gentle run – one that William had taught by demonstration and by using it, the two could maintain for hours.

He had also gained a good sense of direction, taking the sun and hillsides into account, but had learned something more, again at William's teaching. The older lad had told him about the birds and animals having a natural way of getting where they needed to go. 'Let you senses lead you.' This the English lad had learned to do. His chosen place to aim for was, according to this instinct, the ancient ditch where Uncle Emyr had dug up old Roman bones. It was here, Jon Bach decided, William would wait for him because he would be getting tired and would feel it the best place to watch for unusual movement down the fall of the hill. They both knew it to be the best route back, well down the hillside and so out of sight of the path past the rock fissure and cave.

Jonathan let all of his civilised instincts go. He had increased his pace considerably - his own choice. Everything inside him was bent upon finding William and escape. After some minutes of this fast pace, he heard crows squawk a warning. The nests could be seen high over to his left through a break in the trees. He chanced they were the same birds that had let out a warning when Mr Kenton's gun had gone off. If this was the way William had run, the crow's nests would be near the long path cut into the hillside they came down. The boy changed course nimbly, skirted some big brambles and cut a darting path through ferns and bracken to take his route further down the steep hillside – but not too far or he would miss his cousin completely.

All the while as he ran, jumped and twisted a course through the dark wood, Jon Bach could feel the danger in his heart from Kenton and that big gun. He was beginning to think himself lost beyond hope when a twinkle of light from the high sun caught his eye as he leapt a stand of gorse. It took only a flicker of imagery for the boy to see it was the buttress rock not far from the fissure and about two hundred yards higher up the hill. Jon Bach sped on, climbing now as he ran, a harder route until the ragged line indicated the ancient death ditch of the

Twelfth Legion. Just as he had envisaged, William was under cover but sharp eyes were on the look out

'Hey, Jon Bach. Up here. Quick as you like.'

Within a minute the two were together again. William was utterly astonished to hear the younger boy's tale and even more astonished to find him free and unharmed. And then they were off. The enchantment of thicket, ancient wall and nature's darkest corners still burnished by radiant sun-shafts, beams of golden sunlight cutting through the high canopies sped them on, a balm to quickly tiring limbs. They crossed the London road at speed and then up past Gwninger Farm and on up the Rhiwlas, across sheep cropped meadowlands in panting unison. After a break near the little roadway that led down to Hendre Bach cottage, they sprinted the last to see Taid waving cheerfully, smoke from his pipe a little cloud of blue.

Some days later, with both the boys asleep in their beds exhausted by the day's work, William Williams awoke deep into the night to hear Pero barking unexpectedly outside in the cobbled yard. He wasn't alarmed. High above the waxing moon shone in a half clear sky as silvered clouds edged around her beams. The branches of the old oak next to Prince's stable allowed a solitary glinting shaft through, crossing the bedroom like a fine, wispy yellow line to light the knob on his brass bedstead as if it were an orb of glowing gold. Pero, who had eased his clamour started up again. It was not the hard, rapid, excited bark of a dog when a stranger is about the door, but easier, sounding not so much in the mouth as in the throat and carrying as far as a mile when the wind, like tonight, offered no competition.

Sheep dogs are very alert, keen-eared animals. On moonlit nights especially, one will start somewhere. In an instant another will answer, then another - until five, six or more enliven the midnight hours. And throughout this diligence human beings sleep on knowing all is well, for it is a reassuring sound to country folk. Normally William liked to hear the dogs at night, it made him feel safe, sleepy and snug: the *watchmen* were on guard. Moss joined in suddenly, lifting the wild airy sounds across the hillsides from one farm to another, a series of long barks which faded away to a howl; in it, more than a suspicion of the wild ancestral wolf hunting in some trackless forest thousands of years ago.

Unusually, the twelve-year-old was wide awake now, listening intently, his eyes glistening in the moonbeam until it faded away. Nearby the squeal of a rabbit, probably pursued by a weasel cut the night, a sharp, heart-breaking scream of pain from Cae Bach. Then a long silence. Suddenly William realised his unusual ill-feeling was not

94

emanating from the harsh, earthly night-world outside the little farmhouse window, but from inside; from the very room he was laying in.

He pushed back his blankets with their mat-rag coverings - a hill farm version of a patchwork quilt made by Nain - and the moonbeam slowly reappeared again as clouds continued on countless voyages high above. He followed the thin shaft with questioning, alert eyes now. Something was shining and for a moment he was hard put to identify it. The lustre seemed more than simple reflection and as William remembered his friend's silver shilling standing against the little rail at the back of the chest-of-drawers, he realised that it was this old silver coin that was being lit brightly by the moonlight.

Jonathan started to thrash about in the bed next to him, shouting and babbling incomprehensibly. He jumped in shock, yet was out onto the bare floorboards in a second and shaking the younger boy.

'Wake up, Jon Bach. You're having a nightmare! Come on man.'

The nightmare was out of control and in the darkness a flailing arm caught William in the face, throwing him back across his own bed, shock from the blow blotting out the remaining distraught cries. When William regained himself and had stood up, his cousin was sitting up in the little bed, apparently unaware of what had happened. The younger boy lifted his arm, a night silhouette in the silver moonlight. 'Look. Old Silas's shilling!'

William turned to see the coin shining eerily, so brilliant was it that he blinked in surprise. Once again the moonbeam faded to nothing.

'You had a nightmare.' He lit a candle next to the coin.

'No. It was a sign.'

The Welsh lad crossed the bare boards between them carrying the candlestick and sat on his own bed. 'Sign?' William could see Jonathan's chubby, freckled face now, he was white in spite of the soft yellow glow of the candle.

'I saw Dad's aeroplane going down into the sea. I could hear people shouting and a lady scream...'

'It's a bad dream, that's all. Your Dad said in his letter that he would be flying a new passenger plane soon...'

'No. It's a sign. I know it is.' Jonathan's face took on a queer, frightened look. 'I saw it William, a big silver flying-boat. I know, I really know it is going to crash.'

'Did your dad say he would be in a flying-boat, then?'

'No.'

'There you are.'

'There you are what?'

'Well it must be a dream. He would have said if it were a flying-boat, wouldn't he?'

'Why?'

'Why? Don't be daft, Jon Bach. Every pilot wants a go in a flying-boat because they are the biggest planes in the world.'

'No they're not.'

'They are...'

'If I don't do something, my dad will die.'

The two stared at each other in heavy silence. Jonathan's face was regaining its normal colour now and it was clear that he was very serious.

'I think you've gone mad. I'm tired. Will you go to sleep if I blow this candle out?'

The other shook his head. 'I'm not mad, William. I've never had a sign before - 'at least til I came up here. I'm not a witch or anything I just know, that's all,' his eyes twinkled in the candlelight, 'Nain Hafod would understand.' He pointed to the chest-of-drawers. 'Did you see the silver shilling glow? Old Silas said it was magic and I was to visit him if ever I needed help. Well I do now.'

William felt frightened. 'Magic? Don't be so stupid. You are mad. What can Old Silas do for you anyway?'

'He's the only one who can help me. Not Nain, or Taid. Nainy or Taid Hafod, nor anyone.' Jonathan got out of bed. 'I'm going to the Roman temple to ring the bell and Silas will find me - my sign said I must ask for help.'

'It didn't say you've got to ask Old Mad Silas though, did it?'

'No.'

'There you are then. Silas can't help you. Look. I've told you, Squire's mad as a hatter, and goes out at night on a big horse and ...'

'I know all that, William. I know that!' Jonathan's face looked really angry now. ' He caught me in the wood, not you, remember? And he said that if ever I needed help come to the cave and ring the bell.'

William put the candlestick back on the little chest of drawers next to the shilling. The flame fizzled and flickered, casting moving shadows as he struggled desperately for something sensible to say, but his mind was still full of sleep.

'Use your head, man. What can Silas do?'

The English boy moved down the bed and sat face to face with his friend. 'I can't tell you how I know, William, only Deldramena... My dad's plane will go down into the sea very soon and all the people on the plane will die unless I do something.' 'Who's Deldramena?' William gaped.

'Just someone that's all.'

William was scared now, very scared. But his younger cousin's face warned against more questions. 'Nain Hafod had a forewarning in the war. My dad, Dewi was killed when she dreamed it.' He got up and looked out of the window. 'Moon's gone now. Cloud's are acoming.' He sat back on the bed. 'Perhaps you've had a forewarning too...' Then an idea came into his fuzzy head that might just turn things around and get them back to sleep. He grinned impishly. '...But it won't work if you're not Welsh.'

'Welsh?' Do only the Welsh have forewarnings then?'

'We're Celts, aren't we. Mysterious things happen in Wales.'

Jonathan wrinkled his nose and stared at the candle flame. 'Perhaps. But I'm in Wales now.' He folded his arms. 'When I saw Dad's aeroplane going down to the sea, it was as if I was standing on a cliff, looking out across the sky. I saw everything, William!' The chubby face scowled. 'I must go to Silas. He's my friend.'

'Your friend?' Now the Welsh boy was angry at being out played. 'You're mad. You're both mad. I'll wake up Nain and Taid if you go.'

'No you won't.'

William stood up and pulled his pyjamas trousers up. 'Oh yes I will.'

'Oh no you won't, William.'

'Why not?'

'Because you don't want my dad to die. I'm going out through the kitchen.'

William put the candlestick on the bed to see him better and stared. 'The dogs will start.' He was really very scared now. Wide awake scared.

'You can stop them. Do your special call. We can be back in two or three hours.'

'No. Taid will hit us with dobio! I'll not go with you, Jon.'

'Thought so. You're too scared!' Jonathan pulled off his big nightshirt, the pyjamas having given out three weeks before as threadbare and started to get dressed. This was really becoming too much of an insult for the older boy who was as proud as he was clever. A vein of adventure ran through William Williams like gold, it was on par with his sound common sense and the two traits had always fought for supremacy.

'It's pitch black outside. You've only been into Squire's Wood once, you'll never do it alone.' William's face was pleading. 'Wait 'til dawn. We'll go up there together after breakfast...'

The English lad turned, his freckled face clear in the candlelight and he broke into a proud grin. 'Those two hurricane lamps in the shippon where Taid keeps his peat spade and Nain bakes her bread will do. Come on, William. Silas can save my dad. I know he can. He's special. This is going to be the best adventure you've ever been on in your whole life!'

\*     \*     \*

The boys left the stone barn by the back door, the Ladies of Snowdon directly ahead but invisible in the black of night. Cae Bach dropped away quickly and steeply after about twenty yards, once below Hendre Bach farmhouse they skirted around to the left, two hurricane lamps travelling like fireflies across the shrouded hillside towards the newly mettled road which made the lower boundary to Mr Williams's land.

'Put out the lamp, Jon Bach.'

'Why? I can't see much as it is.'

William lifted his hurricane lamp, face stern and eerie. 'Because I said so.' He looked up. 'Moon'll be out soon. We can go just on mine now until it does. Gate's over there.'

They climbed it, handing the remaining illuminated lamp to one another as the long wooden gate creaked under each boy in the silent windless dark, then they hurried off down the pitch black road which ran from the hamlet of Nebo, less than a mile behind them and on down in steep twists to Llanwrst three miles away. The moon, as William had predicted sailed out from her wreath of clouds and shone down on them kindly; William was committed now, if Nain and Taid found out about this escapade the trouble would be unimaginable, Jonathan was so determined upon praying for his father in Old Silas's temple, that William had decided to get it over and done with as soon as possible and return to his warm bed before daybreak - if he could.

'Look lively, Jon. I'll put my lamp out now. Moon's our guide for a while yet.'

Some way down the road, probably more than a mile, for in the soft moonlight it was hard to tell exactly how far they had travelled, William relit his lamp and peered into blackness over a stone wall on the left of the road. Suddenly the English boy could see his friend's face brighten.

'Here it is.' He looked about the road cautiously. 'Light your lamp with these matches and follow me!'

On the other side, a narrow overgrown track disappeared into the undergrowth, its beginnings were lit indeterminately by William's bright lamp.

'This is it. If we follow the path down through the woodland, we'll come out eventually on the Capel Garmon road, in front of Coed Cilcennus,' he stared, 'Cilcennus Wood in the English.'

'I know!'

'From there, it is an easier walk to Squires Wood and the rock passage. Mind this path, it is treacherous enough in the daylight and a fool's errand at night with great drops in places, but we have no choice if we are to keep faith with your forewarning. Keep your lamp out high and do not lose sight of me, Jon Bach. Your life's on it. Come on!'

They moved off. All of their play on the hillsides was now paying a handsome return in a way neither had expected. Sycamore and oak, quickbeam, elm, beech and silver birch, clamouring tendrils of creeper plants, ancient stone walls, gorse and bracken, tree roots and dead logs; all took on the oneness of night. Only their precious hurricane lamps gave the way some half measure of possibility. William was not afraid, even there. He knew every part of the land about; Squire Bellamy's, his family's or the wild open hillsides beyond. Nature held no fear for the Welsh farmer's son, but Old Silas and that ancient temple at night... He was proud of his English cousin. No boy whom he had ever met was as steadfast as Jon Bach. William would never admit to it of course, particularly as Jonathan was more than eighteen months younger than him. And he could sense the fear close behind in the murk of that dark night as Jonathan kept position, close behind and yet as determined as a lion not to be beaten by anything.

They crossed the Capel Garmon road together and entered the less demanding Coed Cilcennus at good pace. Moon was high and it glinted a fine light here and there through the black canopy high above them, but both lamps blazed nonetheless such was the darkness of the woodland floor. Soon Jonathan recognised the small meadow where Old Silas had caught him, eventually letting him go with the silver shilling as a gift, perhaps a token of goodwill he hoped. The boy felt for it in the pocket of his tweed jacket as they hurried along with their wild errand. The land rose again and soon the two were on the gulley-path which climbed and cut its ancient way through dense heartwood.

'Look, there!' William pointed up the path. To the left, about fifty yards ahead loomed the great buttress rock which they had approached from the opposite side to be caught by Kenton, the Squire's gamekeeper. The moon, a globe lamp floating bright above the trees, now lit pieces of mica and quartz which sparkled like powdered glass cast down its sheer, ghostly sides. They entered the crevice, little wider than a man, their animated shadows dancing grotesquely up the high walls like giants before the hurricane lamps and soon the boys were standing once more in the rocky enclosure, diamond stars piercing the black sky-canopy high above them and the black studded oak door of the portico eerie in the gloom of night.

'C'mon. Let's ring the temple bell.' William's whispered words sounded loud in the restricted space.

'It'll be alright. He looks for Frenchies at night or day...' the younger boy grinned nervously, 'but if I ever need help to come here and toll the bell and he would come. So he won't be angry you see?'

William glared. He was not frightened of the dark night in a wild piece of elder land miles from his own isolated home, but of being trapped there like chickens in a pen if the old bell's call was answered. Yet the farm boy knew he had to see it through as he had promised. He felt like a guardian, somehow, a custodian, making good his English cousin's forewarning.

They opened the great door which creaked loudly on its rusting iron hinges, found the rope above the little table inside the entrance and pulled it from the fissure which ran up to the bell tower on the summit of the buttress rock. Putting in every effort, the two then hauled on the long cord for all they were worth, lamps blazing at their feet.

They had been huddled under the portico little more than ten minutes after the first deep knell had rolled out loudly into the cool night air, when Jonathan's keen ears heard a horse's gentle whinny and William's sharp eyes saw the flicker of flame. First came a yellow glimmer to the walls of the crevice-path followed by the sound of careful horse's hooves and dancing shadows, then Old Silas appeared suddenly from the cleft like a phantom. He walked out into the high rock wall enclosure guardedly, leading his big white stallion, a flaming torch held high with the reins.

'Who calls Silas from his duties?' The torch was in his left hand and, at the same time, both boys saw the old-fashioned powder and ball pistol pointing at them from his right. His voice was coarse, but not in expression, for gentry ran through it like silver thread.

## Eleven

Jonathan got to his feet immediately. 'Please sir, it's me, Jonathan - the orphan boy.' His voice sounded weird in the high-walled rocky chasm where they stood.

The white, ghostly face stared hard from under the tricorne hat. 'And who's the boy with you, pray?'

'My friend, William. I am living on William's farm until my father returns for me. Father is going to die very soon far out at sea and I come for your help, if you will give it, sir.' The strange figure stood quite still. William had never seen the apparition they called Old Silas so close to before. He was stunned. Then, without further ado the man turned and placed the torch in a cleft in the rock wall and climbed back on his great white horse, the ends of his silk tail-coat flicking out as he cocked a leg over the saddle, the buckle of his lifted shoe drawing brightness from the torchlight. He bade him move nearer the portico and sat staring at the intruders, pistol unwavering at arms length. Suddenly, as if making some private decision of importance, the strange figure climbed back down again and tied the beautiful stallion's reins to a small bush which was growing out of the craggy rock wall opposite the entrance. The stallion blew through his nostrils, shook his proud head and Silas walked across to the portico, lowered the hammer of the pistol and pushed it back into the top of his white breeches. Both boys stood side by side, their blazing lamps standing on the marble floor at the feet of the fluted pillars.

'You said your father was a ship's captain when I saw you before.'
'Yes sir.'
'And his ship has floundered?'
'I had a dream.'
'A premonition, by gad? When?'
'Tonight, sir.' Jonathan indicated to William. 'My friend said he would help me come to you, because you promised to help me if I had no one else to turn to.'

'And you have no one?' The voice has eased a little now, the gruffness a background and they saw his old eyes glinting in the torchlight.

'No. No one who can help before the night is out. But my forewarning said I must ask for help if my father is to be saved. And you are my friend!'

The white, powdered face stared, eyes moving first from one young face and then to the other. 'Your friend?' Why say you that?'

'Only a friend promises to help when no one else will...'

Silas put his hands on his hips, white silk ruffles almost covering them. 'This is not a Christian Church, young wayfarer, but a temple to the great god Mithras. Have you heard of Mithras?'

'Yes, sir.'

The whitened face smiled. 'How say you?'

'William told me all about him. How he was worshipped by the Roman soldiers and everything.'

Careful eyes turned to William. 'You know a lot for a farmer's boy...'

'I can read, sir. And I have good ears for tales and legends.'

'Indeed.'

They could see the man clearly in the lamps now. His face was made up with powder and rouge like an old-fashioned dandy in the history books, his beautiful, immaculate clothes could have come from the old painting in the manor house as the stories told. The face, aristocratic and proud, was clearly that of Squire Bellamy, they knew him from Church, standing at the lectern or in the front pew, but the man scowling before them now was totally different; far beyond that contrived by clothes, pistol or horse. He had a different disposition, everything was different, much more than the wiles of a clever actor, as if the rightful owner of the ageing body had been temporarily driven out and replaced by a different soul; perhaps, thought Jonathan, someone long dead from the gentry, or perhaps even one of Squire Bellamy's ancestors.

'I am fain to help you with such a tale - but if it be merely a tale, you boys will feel my shoe buckle at your backsides, for I am yet to be convinced you are nothing more than common scallywags!'

The two stared at one another.

'More! I wish to know much more. What ship does your father sail, me lad, and what are his credentials of passage? The Hudson Bay Company, perhaps?'

Jonathan's wide eyes remained fastened on the strange man. He did not understand his queer talk, but got enough of its gist to offer a strong reply. 'Sir. My father sails a special ship. The first to fly across the seas at great speeds. I know little because he captains the very first of its type and with luck he could make the first passage to Europe in the quickest time ever. In my dream I saw his ship lose its speed, then a great storm come out of the east to destroy her.'

'Is your father racing against the chronometer or fast clippers?'

'Only time, sir. They are completely alone.'

As Old Silas paused to think, he caught sight of a nervous glance between the boys.

'And what say you, boy? William, isn't it?'

'Yes sir.' William looked across to his friend again and tried to conceal a mounting fear, for terror was now stalking so close he was at the point of making a dash for the narrow path that instant, but the fearsome man would be mostly in his way whichever way he ran. Even with such dread, the Welsh farm boy still could not leave Jon Bach to this crazy spectre he had managed to out manoeuvre for many years of cat and mouse. 'My father was a soldier in the Great War. My grandmother had a forewarning that he was going to die in October 1918 and he did. It happened at the same time as she had her dream. I believe in Jonathan, sir. He is good and honest and if he says he knows his father will die soon because of his dream, then I believe him. I wouldn't have helped him find you otherwise.'

The three stared at each other. Old Silas's flickering torch throwing dancing shadows from the other side of the rocky opening. Their two hurricane lamps, hoop-handled and barred answering with steady light.

'What say you then of this, boys? Would it not pain you and your families if I were to offer a prayer of contrition from this pagan edifice to the great god Mithras - goodly as it may be...' he looked deep into their young faces, as if seeking a reaction, but the boys did not move, '...this ancient temple, where Legionaries of Rome once bowed their heads. And what of the stalwart god Mithras himself? A god now long forgotten by mankind, perhaps? Does he still stalk the world? Awaiting petition from the likes of us? Or is his existence, like this old place, now but a faint memory? Are ye asking help from Mithras by earnest prayer? How say ye?'

The torch flickered and the careful eyes under the tricorne hat burned once more; first at Jonathan and then at William.

'I don't mind if we pray to your god, Mithras.'

'My god?'

'Yes, sir.' Jonathan looked scared. But determination was clear in his eye.

'I have a cross,' William suddenly blustered, now terrified at some pagan ritual way beyond his knowing being enacted. Then his stance fell to a sudden pleading look, which seemed to shake the aristocrat from his harsh bearing. 'My father made it at the Front before he was killed. Would it help us, sir?' The boy opened his shabby jacket and lifted the cross from around his neck and put it into Silas's soft hand. It was made from an ancient piece of dark oak, about two inches long by one and a quarter wide with a perfect half lap joint at the middle. Although rustic by the standards of some, the rood pleased both eye and touch; a simple clasped chain ran through a tiny metal eyelet at the top.

'A fine piece of scrimshaw work and no mistake.' The whitened face lifted a slight smile. 'Your father was a soldier, then?'

William nodded.

The face eased to melancholy and the eyes glazed over as if almost remembering something just out of reach. 'I think I remember a soldier...a long way off now...he was a brave soldier so they said. A brave soldier who served a great king in a terrible war where uncounted thousands of brave men died...' Old Mad Silas stood with his head bowed, staring at the cross in his hand, the cockade in his hat clear in the lamplight, the foppish clothes no longer needed to make him special.

'Please, sir, will my father's cross help us? Can we go in now?'

Silas looked up, wetness to his eye. The faith ye place in me as your guide is heartening in this world beset by woe. I am fain obliged to help ye. But it is not my place to choose the path.' A pause fell across the enclosure, then his old head turned suddenly, stern again, as if once more a personal, but this time irrevocable decision had been made.

The boys felt shock but stood firm in their spirits.

'Let us enter the temple and talk further. I shall then see what is to be done.'

They chorused careful agreement. If he was mad, and there seemed little doubt of it now, at least Silas was behaving much like the friend Jon Bach seemed to believe he was. William had lifted spirits as well, hoping that perhaps the forewarning would soon be observed and they would be fast away.

The big iron ring turned to Silas' hand, partly hidden by white silk ruffles at his sleeves and the black studded oaken door swung its creaking path open.

He put his tricorne hat down on the little table just inside the door, lit the candle in its silver holder and worked his way to the cone-shaped lamps mounted on the four pillars. The head of Mithras which had looked so supernatural before, the halo of daylight from the crevice behind now gone, had strangely lost none of its mysticism with the night, gaining cold life from the burning of the oil lamps. They crossed the mosaic floor together, the two boys, one on each side and slightly behind Old Silas, his gentry head crowned with powdered, snow-white flowing hair, and for the first time the man's proud, haughty manner was subdued.

He got down carefully on ageing knees before the life size stone head set on the marble-topped high altar table. The boys stood silently near the entrance watching him as he spoke some words in Latin which they did not understand. Silas was visibly struggling under the weight of his emotions now. Squire Bellamy had been aroused from deepest slumber in the aristocratic head, a mere flicker away from this wild trespasser who still held sway over his body.

After the peacock man rose from his knees, William found himself clutching his father's cross deep in his ragged trouser pocket and unexpectedly drawn into a silent veneration of his own, as if trying to keep the frightening statue head of Mithras from turning to stare at Jonathan and him. There was a definite atmosphere in the cavern now, it seemed to have come from nowhere, a strange warm feeling. In spite of his puzzlement, William remained as still and composed as his pumping heart would allow. It felt like Sunday morn when the family were all getting ready for Church together; or harvest time down on the lowland farms when they joined with other families who came from far and wide to celebrate crops safely gathered and join in happy society. Only the flickering light about the marble pillars and glitterings from mica in the cave walls held anything like change, yet that was no change at all.

Mithras stared ahead, his stony eyes cold. The air, all about them seemed to be enveloped by the pleasant feeling, like Christmas eve, everyone soon to be lifted by presents and the holiday tomorrow morn. William could not understand the change and felt anxiety grow among the warmth, but also an overwhelming determination not to mess up anything for Jon Bach. He stood completely still.

The nobleman bade them sit down on the ancient bench seats beneath the deity statuettes on the left side of the cave.

'Jonathan...' The old face looked kindly as he sat next to him, different somehow as if the Squire was struggling to return. 'You carry a grievous burden for one so young. A father who captains a ship soon to be in the direst peril. He is I am sure a good man to have raised such a fine young son. But he is only a man like me. I wish time to dwell herein and make my peace as best I may with my maker before I try to help you. But we have little time left...'

The wind had risen slightly and was now playing about the bell tower high above them, its sound haunting the fissure running down into the cave entrance like a breeze in some great manor house chimney. Jonathan lifted his eyes and looked up at the figure beside him. A tear was coursing the white cheek, marking a line through the rouge and face powder. Unexpectedly the aristocratic figure rose, turning toward the altar as if again he had suddenly made up his mind upon something known only to him. Both boys had noticed the change in his demeanour and now, as he spoke again, they recognised clearly the voice of Squire Bellamy.

'Let it please you Almighty God to release this boy from his onerous burden and bring his father and all those in his charge home safely to port. I am also aware that this great ship, flying across the seas on great wings of speed, carries a man who, in his turn, is carrying the greatest evil. I do not know how this knowledge is in my head, only that I beg your forgiveness of all men, even one such as he, so that we may all try again for the true path of your righteousness and love.' He bowed his old head solemnly. 'Amen.'

They all remained quiet and still.

'We have done our best, we three and are now waiting upon Grace from a better place than this harsh world. A glorious warmth fills me now where there should only be cold antiquity.'

They nodded silently.

'Good. It bodes well for us all. William. Please take your young friend home now. See that both he and you get safely into your beds. I wish to stay here quite alone now and....' The whitened head bowed. 'Leave me. I will do what I can for your father and his brave ship.'

Soon they were at the entrance, helping to shut the dark oaken door. A glimmer of dawn would be marking the sky in a short while. The boys could not speak more than a few words of direction to one another until they reached the far end of Coed Cilcennus, such was their emotions, hoping to get back before empty beds were noticed.

For much of the climb back up to Hendre Bach, William, who regained his spark quickly, chided his young English cousin about the secret gift Jonathan now supposedly bore within him. Old Silas, or was it Squire Bellamy, had made that plain enough before their final parting at the big oak door. Some measure of a madman's fantasy, perhaps? They didn't know. Jonathan made little comment. Only that his father's dangerous flight across the Atlantic Ocean was now being overseen by Jesus. Of this he had no doubt at all. The happy conviction lifted weary feet as they tramped along the steeply climbing moonlit road. The forewarning had been well observed.

As for me, I had allowed Squire Bellamy enough of himself to function as if in a waking dream. Yet he was alive to every moment. So in a very real and truthful sense Bellamy had asked for everything from his Maker with sincerity. A Doorkeeper can never manipulate without compassion for each human soul.

# Twelve

## Eight Days Later

Farm work had been unrelenting but William had managed to get Jon Bach and himself some time down by the little river where they had seen the otters play in the off-shoot pool. Catching trout by hand had been the idea but William seemed distracted and was in a strange mood.

Soon after drinking some refreshing *nant* water from a bubbling part of the little river they were on their way again. The boys turned through tall ferns, ancient weeds and prolific plant growth of all kinds, William looking up through the tree canopy for the sun's glitter to guide him. They were going further into the greater part of the forest than either of them had been before.

'Where we going?'

William pushed his shock of dark curly hair back and arced a hand across a stand of tall foxgloves so that they bobbed lightly, releasing some buzzing insects in a cloud of summer warmth. 'I don't know, Jon Bach.' His dark eyes searched back and forth carefully, ill-ease just visible for the first time since they had been up to Old Silas' lair. 'I have never been here before. I just need to know...'

Suddenly he shot off through the pathless undergrowth like a ferret after some prey. Jon Bach was at his heels in seconds. But soon they were slowed by the tight, interwoven wild plants and tall fauna of the untrespassed forest. Ten minutes later the bright beams of sunlight that had reached them indicated a meadow ahead which fell steeply at first to reveal a few ancient trees near to the centre of a lush, uncropped sward of deep green. The place was completely new to William. He stepped out, that long fingered hand above his eyes and lanky frame turning carefully about to take measure of their find.

'C'mon. I've never been in this part of Squire's Wood before.'

'It's more like a jungle to me.'

'Look lively, Jon Bach. I don't want that game keeper to catch us again.'

The two shot off, skirting the few knarled old elm trees in the middle of the lush meadow and headed for a tiny opening set into what looked like even more dense woodland on the far side. Running crisp, light steps they moved silently like animals in natural unison. If out of sight and few feet away you would have heard no sound of footfall, such was their lightness of step. The tiny path now took a wandering route steeply upward, struggling precariously between a steep vertical cliff and the Afon Gallt-y-Gwg which lay well to their right; birch and alder trees hiding the river's chuckling presence.

They came to a small defile, little more that a gentle dip in the ground about thirty feet long which was full of the most beautiful flowers William had ever seen in his life. They were large, climbing the side of the cliff as far as he could see and strewn ahead in white and gold profusion. They seemed to be twinkling gently like jewelled ornaments in the vivid sunshine. William looked back at Jonathan who was panting; his freckled cheeks vivid, sweat lining his glistening face. They both felt strange about themselves and the extraordinary glowing scene before them. The younger boy espied some large mushrooms and cried out.

William took no notice. Standing stock still he continued to survey the scene in some wonder. The place seemed to have enchantment. He turned back, staring at the way they had come and the peculiar feeling weakened the further he looked back through the huddle of wild vegetation. Those long, clever fingers ran through his dark curls again, trying to clear his mind from strange delight. The Welsh farm boy had never experienced anything like this before in all his wild roaming across mountain or moor.

Together they ran on pell mell as if drawn forward. William could only conclude that Jon Bach's stamina must have improved suddenly and hugely, for it took everything he had in him to catch up. Yet try as he might, the older, larger boy could not overtake. A race was on.

Jonathan had lost all sense of danger now; he felt drawn to follow the path without any care. They scrambled for supremacy but Jonathan held onto his lead like a fox with hounds at his heels. Neither could guess how long they ran, only that it must have been for a very long while. The path twisted, rose and fell seemingly without end, the farm boy calling out all the while for a slowing of pace. But Jon Bach became progressively faster, jumping higher and so very far it seemed to William, giving out wild cries of exhilaration. William closed and for every leap they both sailed further and further through the air.

Abruptly the two shot out into a tiny opening running like madmen and stopped suddenly, for standing a short distance away at the foot of a tall cliff stood Squire Bellamy, arms folded across his red silk tail-coat; strange, yet kindly eyes staring out from under the tricorne hat. There was no sign of his great horse, Butterscotch.

Slim, gangling William showed as much fear as he ever would, for where now stood the squire, also stood Mad Silas - sooner or later. A sudden determination shone from William's dark eyes, for this seemed like a very neat trap to him. He turned ready to protect Jon Bach and run, black hair glistening with sweat. Before he could take a step Squire Bellamy's gentle voice rang out.

'I'm pleased to see you boys again. In fact I...' the gentry figure paused, '...I believe I have guided you here...If I have...' rheumy blue eyes flickered and his face, with its fair complexion and gentle air that had been bred from agreeable living and pleasant company began to tremble. His mouth twitched appreciably; then a totally different creature filled the noble body to immediately appraise the two boys with interest - same nobility of bearing, same bodily stance; but now with stern, immeasurable depths. Silas continued to stare at them without speaking. They could see it was the madman alright. Fear seemed to be held at bay for the moment as if their alarm was being willed into submission. His arm lifted authoratively, silk ruffles at the sleeve and a white, diamond ringed finger was pointed at Jonathan.

Those once immaculate clothes observed by Silas when the boy had first arrived; tweed jacket, short grey trousers, school socks and polished shoes were now either hanging by threads, in tatters, or badly scuffed. Jonathan was still panting; his freckled young face had a scratch from the pell mell which had bled. A shock of light brown hair now much longer was nearly in his widely-opened brown eyes. Silas took every detail in very quickly. Jon Bach's open expression, innocent of all danger, still shone back at the wild man as happy and cheerful as a crackling fire on Christmas morn. William on the other hand was looking for a way out as quickly as he could like a cornered animal.

'Please sit down.' The nobleman's arm swept round again to three great stones behind them, smooth boulders that were shaped with indentations as if by wind and rain over the centuries. William reacted with surprise. He did not remember them as they had run up. A glance at Jonathan confirmed his fear. Two of the boulders were set together near the cliff face, the third stood over by the path. As William gaped, bright sunshine came out from a single cloud high above and Silas asked them to sit once more. The boys did as they were bid and Silas settled himself on the boulder by the pathway, flicking out the tail-coat as if an everyday event. As they sat still, whatever ease that had filled Jonathan to overflow now came at William in great waves. But he fought it hard, keeping himself in contention and alert as much as he could muster.

'This lovely world you know so well, William; and which you too have learned about in recent months, Jonathan is alive. This whole world we call Mother Earth. She is a living creature just like you or me, a

**111**

creature who thinks feels and sees.' The tricorne was removed and placed on the ground. Powdered hair fastened low with a blue bow on the nape of his neck flicked out over a small silk collar as he turned this way and that, pointing at trees and plants all around, and commenting upon their beauty and vitality. As he did so wild birds appeared and began to fly around him, some settling near his feet, others among the lovely golden flowers close to the path.

'Mother Earth watches us all. She watches life's progress, in particular the great tribe of tiny living creatures struggling and working across her vast and wonderful body. That tribe you and I know as the human race.'

He smiled. 'William. I know that you distrust me. This I understand. Under the circumstances you are sensible to think that way. But I have brought you here – yes into a sort of trap as you suspected – to explain who I am and why I am here. I mean neither of you any harm, nor could I do you harm even if I wished it...' He stopped, waiting for a reply, but only received careful stares in return.

Suddenly, Jonathan with a look of pleading turned to William; the older boy simply put a finger to his lips for silence.

'I am a Doorkeeper, *Drysorion* as you say in Welsh, William. I am a servant of Mother Earth, this great planet, like many other Doorkeepers who do her bidding. We have no bodies of our own, yet we can inhabit the body of any person at will - as I do now. Your good squire sleeps within this body and will come to no harm as long as I possess him.'

Once again the now sharp blue eyes searched for reaction but none came. Silas laughed and shook the noble head; leaning forward he lifted the ring finger again. In that instant the boys felt their minds opening, as if a lock on childhood had been turned.

'Do you understand how a tree, a great tree, like an oak or elm will grow from a tiny acorn or kernel? Do you know where the vigour comes from to make that mighty tree?'

The boys sat quiet still. Once again I surveyed them as they remained speechless, knowing that it was my duty to fashion honeyed words, durable as the oak tree itself for the founding of a reality in their young minds - an absolute truth that the greatest scholars since the times of Ancient Greece had never imagined, even in their wildest dreams. And this candour, beyond knowledge of the greatest of men was now to be set into the heads of mere boys aged ten and twelve years of age by me. I felt awed and anxious by it, but She had demanded it. I must obey. This was a potent burden to be transferred to ones so young. And so, I continued in hope that the quality She Herself had claimed was in these scraps of children, whom I had come to love, would prove well founded.

'The vigour to make the tree grow and live comes from within the Earth Herself. It is called pure energy by some. I am merely created from a small part of that boundless energy used to make a tree, an animal or a man. She chose to make me - a creature of great power like the wind or sea – but only to serve Her will. I have no body, but this does not make me any less alive or real. For I am pure energy under Her dominion.

Each one of us has tasks to complete as we live. For people, lifetimes are all that is given. I am given time itself to use. My tasks never finish. That is how I have been made. And I am content with that, for that is how all Doorkeepers live.'

I looked hard at each boy in turn and believed that they were now open and ready for me to continue. Then I drew a long, silent breath from within my human host, more for his cerebral refreshment which I was using, rather than physical need, and continued.

'A long time ago, when Mother Earth was young, a time before time itself, the first race of human beings arose. They were just like people today, under Her love, then as now. But unlike today, those people knew the Earth was alive and aware of their existence. They respected Her and obeyed Her natural laws. They called their homeland Ansaurius. For Mother Earth, a billion years can be like a minute. A minute like a billion years. This civilisation grew into a great and wonderful empire. An empire that would eventually stretch from east to west, north to south; a world united as one: Mother Earth and Her Children.'

\*     \*     \*

Silas lifted his hands and out of a narrow opening in the cliff to their right came a sudden whoosh of light. It twinkled and wove like living lace, a twisting, translucent mist curtain, which entwined itself around Silas' legs so that his stockings and part of his white breeches could not be seen clearly. Quickly the embracing mist grew and as it did, so a wonderful sound filled them, not just in their ears but within their whole being. It was as if they had heard such an echo all their lives in another consciousness but never in the time-space of now; a high humming glow of sound, like a choir practising in a great cathedral and achieving the perfect note for a few seconds before an anthem would start. Yet it was even more extraordinary than that.

They could hardly see Silas now, he and they were surrounded by what looked like tiny glistening wings; moving, interlacing, merging, showering split-seconds of tiny, brilliant coloured light all around their rock walled platform. The boys could still see his rouge and powdered face, but little more; such was their encirclement. William and Jonathan had been able to comprehend so much, taking everything that Silas had taught them as if at their mother's knee. From somewhere came the spirit of their kindly old squire, words in their heads echoed magically, saying over and over again, 'do not be afraid. You will be safe. I will be with you.'

'Put your hands out boys.'

The two started suddenly. Tiny creatures were now coming quickly out of the lace-mist, so close to their glowing faces that the instant of it made the boys blink. Tiny ladies with green and golden clothes which seemed to have been grown, rather than made. Handsome, tiny winged men arrived in glittering golden chain mail suits that ran from chest to knee, dark belts with tiny daggers set in them, some escorting their ladies away courteously, others gambolling like children. To and fro' they darted, all on minuscule but powerful gossamer wings. They smiled before the boys' astonished eyes, then in a twinkling of those eyes male and female were gone among the weaving, glittering mists.

'Faeries these. Handmaidens of nature some have said - people who were fortunate enough to espy them.' Silas nodded firmly. 'But you boys must know the real truth; for all faeries are Handmaidens of this world, our planet Earth.' He lifted the noble head. 'Fear not. These are Her enchantment creatures who help with special errands when She deems it so. Put your hands out again, boys.'

Together both William and Jon Bach stretched out an open hand. William his right, Jonathan his left, William's hand was directly above Jonathan's. Instantly a faerie flew to them and stood on William's palm so they could both see her bright beauty. They were entranced.

'This is Lightflame. She is to guide you on your passage.'

The faerie bowed. She had long golden hair, a green dress with the tiniest flowers decorating its waist and hem; others were set in her shining hair, so small that they could hardly be made out. Her face was a healthy brown as if she had lived a lifetime in sunshine; tiny eyes were glowing like miniature diamonds. Lightflame was the most beautiful creature William had ever seen in his life. Beauty seemed to fill her to overflow. Both boys' mouths were agape. The ragged Welsh son-of-the-soil knew at that moment, when he grew up, he would search the whole world for a lady as fair as she, a human lady he could love forever. William could hardly feel her on his hand and full of inquisitiveness he leaned further and further forward until she flew back into the mist which they now saw was made up from thousands of other cavorting faeries in an endless band of light.

'Do not attempt to touch Lightflame, William. She is far quicker than you could ever dream...'

The faerie returned smiling teasingly and spoke words that neither of the boys could hear.

'You will find that her voice will carry to you as your test moves forward.' Mad Silas' face, stern but encouraging made for a smile.'

Slowly the two leaned towards Lightflame and they heard her voice for the first time. It was like the tinkling of a tiny waterfall into a tiny pool. A joy to their ears.

'We must leave now. I will lead you,' she cried as if shouting out across a chasm. 'Keep close to me and you will see Ansaurius.'

'You hear her then?'

The two nodded at the anxious face staring at them through the swirling faerie-mist.

'Where are we going?'

Mad Silas smiled freely for the first time. 'Why Lightflame has just told you. We go to Ansaurius of course!'

Before William or Jon Bach could form a sensible reply, the band of weaving light began to move. In no more than a few seconds the faerie host had vanished, taking the boys and Silas with them. The sun shone over the little rock-walled dell. The birds flew off to the sounds of fluttering and birdcall, leaving the gentle woodland grove to a windless silence.

## Thirteen

There were few cars and trucks then - no mobile phones, iPods, laptops, webcams, junk food, carbon foot prints or pollution. This it is well to remember, for such spiritual gifts as Owain Williams and his family had remained close to them; a powerful link with the fertile Earth — Her trees, plants, animals and birds all around. But the coming of the computer forty years later signalled the weakening of humanity's link with Mother Earth who is undoubtedly your physical benefactor.

The computer is not at fault — it is a huge tool for the benefit of humanity. But it beguiles. People lose themselves within its enticement and are being charmed away into a world not quite real — like a song set in the human mind which cannot be ignored; like a drum beat which resonates loudly, running faster and faster and to ignore it is to be left behind in the unreasoned race for progress. But there is another rhythm too, a real, strong and powerful rhythm which is witness to a Spirit pulsing throughout the cosmos and through every fibre of the Earth. For humanity this beat is barely audible and heard not at all to those lost in technology. As a Doorkeeper, I can hear this rhythm of the Earth's Great Spirit whenever I wish. I just listen. The unbreakable rhythm is linked with the seasons, tides, phases of the moon and the movements of all celestial bodies. That rhythm is as real as you are and to lose contact with it breaks the bond between Mother Earth and humanity. That is what happened to the first race of humanity so long ago and why She allowed it to perish.


In that same instant of transport the scene before their eyes was replaced by a feeling of drier warmth and the boys found themselves standing on the most beautiful green hill. The three looked up into a cloudless blue sky; there the faerie hosts were circling in a fine weaving cloud, like many thousands of tiny birds readying themselves for migration.

'Watch now...' Silas pointed upwards and the moving cloud swirled and then vanished into a tiny fixed point of nothing high above. 'Ha!' He shouted loudly, blue eyes a twinkle. 'They're gone me lads. Gone but they'll return when we are ready for them. Have no fear.'

Already William was surveying the scene all around. It was the most beautiful country he had ever seen. They were on the top of a long high hill, surrounded by similar undulating lush grassland, stands of trees and woodlands were dotted as far as he could see. High about bluebirds swooped and played. He could hear them. Not far away was a rough hewn wooden post with a gold coloured bell at its top hanging from a black wrought iron hook. Further down the hillside peeked the top of what looked like a strange little house. He turned this way and that and gasped.

'What think you, William Williams? Does this seem perhaps familiar?' Silas had lifted the tricorne as seemed to be his way when he wanted to ponder or hear reply. A light breeze was lifting wisps of his powdered hair and he smiled broadly, showing the gold tooth.

William turned towards Silas' resplendent figure for a moment, and then back as if finding himself party to some clever trick. 'Yes I do, sir. But I don't know why.'

The man nodded. 'You are seeing your homeland, William, the farm and the lands all around it long, long ago – as it was when time was young – at the time of Ansaurius. These are only the bare bones of the land you know but with flesh of the Earth upon them that is sweet and abundant.' He sighed. 'So long ago and –'

'This is Ansaurius?' The farm boy looked incredulous. 'Thousands of years ago?'

'Billions...'

The dumbfounded silence was broken by Jonathan. 'What's that down there?' He was pointing and looking very frightened. A path meandered down the gentle hillside towards a cottage which was partly hidden by a sturdy old yew tree near to the bottom. The cottage roof, as much as they could see of it, had what looked like large dark brown tiles, the lower edge of each tile was shaped into three of four curves so that it gave the distinct impression to Jonathan at least, of being a sort of giant toy – looking like a gingerbread house.

Silas put his hat on and gave one of his assertive nods. 'That's the Watch Cottage where Jebridiah looks out for travellers.'

The boys chorused who's Jeb-ri-diah but Silas merely smiled. 'Come,' he said gruffly, and they set off down the path. 'You shall meet the Watchtaker now.'

The yew tree was huge, multi-fingered tendrils fell everywhere around the great dark trunk which seemed to be guarding the approach. As the little group got nearer, they could see the cottage walls were light brown, rather like freshly toasted bread, but a closer inspection showed a finish just like tree bark, gentle and soft looking, but tree bark nonetheless. The windows were striking too. William stared in wonder as Jon Bach looked around. Each was a light golden brown in colour and looking like a huge transparent leaf, but shaped perfectly to fit into the particular cavity for which it had been created. One window was partly open, the sun reflecting brightly on its dusky brown hue. The whole window seemed to be bent and was kept open against a natural inclination, as if it would snap lightly shut all on its own when released.

'Hello me dears. What be you doing down here on such a day as this?' The voice was owned by a short, muscular man who had appeared out of nowhere. He was sporting dark brown pork chop sideburns and had a ruddy complexion. His rustic look seemed to be worn with pride, the middle of his head was bald but the remaining hair on either side was vigorous and quite long, as if making up for the loss elsewhere. It complimented his sideburns admirably. If there had been a moustache to add to his description, which there was not, it would have been the highest of moustaches imaginable; for he had a noticeably short nose. His appearance was completed with waistcoat, red neckerchief, brown leather trousers held up with a belt and braces over a check shirt.

'Don't you recognise me, Jeb?'

The little man laughed out loud. A big raucous laugh rather like Silas'. 'Now how could that possible be? I can't see who is inside that aristocratic head, can I? Name please, me beauty. And who's the poor devil you have chosen to reside with today then?'

Silas put his arms out as if welcoming an old friend. 'Name is Drysorion as you surely remember me…'

'Ah.' They fell into each others arms hugging like brothers.

'Not too hard. My host is a delicate soul and will not take lightly to being squashed or bruised.'

'Is that so.' Jeb pulled away, looking at the boys. 'Who are these two fine fella me lads, then? Part of your latest venture?'

'None of your business. We've come for a look round your humble cot.'

'Short visit, then?'

'That it is. These boys have never been to Ansaurius before.'

Jebridiah's careful eyes swung across first to William where he noted the ragged son-of-the-soil appearance, torn waistcoat and holed shirt, then on to Jonathan who didn't look much better. 'Couple of tough uns you got here by the look of it.'

'They'll do. You know I don't waste time on ill-formed errands.'

The Watchtaker lifted a brawny arm in the direction of a little doorway which was surrounded by lovely blue and yellow flowers set among the greenest leaves. 'Enter then, and be welcome.'

Inside a corridor was lit with a gentle light that felt homely. The boys could see five doors, although the passage turned at the end. The walls were light green in colour, looking just like fine tree bark, soft and warm to the touch. They were invited to touch, look and ask any questions they liked. The ceiling was quite high and where a picture rail would have run around a posh room back in Wales, there was a long bulge, as if a narrow piece of wood had been buried there just under the surface, and then finished off smoothly. From above this the soft light was emitted, so that its source could not be seen.

'Why are the lights on in the daytime?' William was really intrigued and pointed at the light bars.

Jeb smiled. 'To show you young rascals, I suppose.' He touched the wall in a circular motion and the light went out on that wall.'

'Wow.'

'How do you do that?' Jonathan was rubbing the wall vigorously.

'No. No, young 'un. Gently, now. Look,' he used his finger to describe a small circle, 'see, the light comes on again. Now you try.'

Before he could touch the wall again William had beat him to it. He drew a circle as instructed and the light went out.

Jeb and Silas laughed as one by one the light was turned on and off by small fingers tracing careful circles on the gentle wall.

William had a smile on his face for the first time and pushed his curls back, dark eyes twinkling. 'How does it work, sir?'

'This house has been grown in the earth.'

The boys stared and said nothing for a few moments.

'Grown?' They chorused.

'Yes. It takes as long as a year to become like this. You both live in the country? What happens in the spring when the first crocuses appear? Have you not seen them close their petals when it is cold, and open them in the sunshine?' He looked carefully at their faces. 'What makes a salmon swim against the current of a mighty river to spawn? Or an ant gather with thousands of its fellows to build a nest? Do you know where the sixth sense comes from to tell them to do this? The answer is simple: Mother Earth guides every one of Her creatures, whether they be large small or tiny, for we all belong to Her. She tells the crocus to close its petals, the salmon to return to the place of its birth and the tiny ant to build his nest.'

'But that is just instinct, sir...'

'Instinct is another word for the Earth acting as a mother, William. Mother Earth helps every one of her children to gain life however humble and to survive for as long as they may, for She and all Her Children are really one huge living entity. There are lines in the ground which are used to channel Her life-energy to us all. They run through this land to many parts. You can't see the lines, even if you dig deep, but they are there just the same.'

Silas joined in. 'Where the boys come from, they know of these lines in myth and legend only. No one understands how to use Spey anymore. And do you know, Jeb, they use a similar word for them, they call them ley lines!'

The watchtaker shook his whiskered head. 'Bless me boots. It's like we always say my friend; if something works, it will cross all time to come around again and again.'

The Watchtaker turned back to the boys. 'In the same way as the crocus knows to open its petals, Mother Earth will let a house pod use the ground where it has been planted to turn the soil and vegetation into a house.'

Both boys seemed to be a little brighter but said nothing for a while until Jonathan spoke up.

'But there isn't the right sort of stuff in the ground to make a cottage like this.' There was a puzzled gleam in his eye.

'Is there enough *stuff* as you call it in the ground to make a big tree? Dig in the ground, Jonathan. Is there bark, sap, wood or fragile leaves to be seen?'

Jeb smiled kindly at their innocence. 'So why not a natural house like this, made of the Earth's raw materials?'

William nodded a little. Jonathan just stared.

'Follow me.' He beckoned and they hurried along the corridor to a small recess in the wall. He pulled open a little door near the floor which was rather like the leaf windows they had seen outside, except this one was not transparent. Inside were two pods growing out of the wall, rather like squat mushrooms. Jebridiah pulled one away with some effort, it made the sort of sound that a boot makes when lifted out of mud. When he let go of the little door, it sprang back of its own accord to fit into the wall recess silently. He offered the house pod to the boys and Jonathan not wanting to be out done took it carefully. It was indeed like a mushroom, but with a hard core just under a soft, pliable surface which felt like velvet. It felt quite heavy too.

'So what does it do, Mr Jeb?'

'If somebody wants another cottage like this, yes? He'll plant a house pod in the ground. But there is much more to do than that, boys which you might see one day perhaps. This pod is a record of everything about the house, just like our crocus, or any other plant, for everything living has its own pattern built into it, and by planting the house pod in the right way, She will know exactly what we want Her to grow.'

121

'Please sir,' William tugged at the Jeb's braces, 'but who is *She*?'

'The stocky man turned, squatted down on his haunches and put large, calloused hands gently on both boys' shoulders. His face took on a kindly, almost pained expression as of one trying hard not to be too patronising to children who were clearly very ignorant. 'She is Mother Earth, me dears. Our world. She is the soul of this planet we call the Earth. You both have souls, don't you?'

They made for acceptance with a smile.

'Well, She has a soul too and is alive, just like you young fellows,' he gave them the gentlest shake and turned his head to Silas, pork chop sideburns lifting among the neckerchief and his broad shoulder. 'Is that not so, me beauty?'

Silas nodded almost sternly. 'That it is.'

'Come on. I'll show you what happens to a house pod if it's not used up quickly.' He stood easily and Jonathan put the pod into his outstretched hand.

Jebridiah led the way to the first room off the corridor, near to the front. The door opened onto a fair sized kitchen. A good, sturdy deal table with four wooden rather rustic chairs were in the middle, cupboards ran along three walls, on the far side two leaf windows were sprung wide open and sun shone through onto twinkling mugs and plates set on hooks and racks under the cupboards. Beneath the window was a large stone sink. The walls and back light looked just the same. They all trooped over to the sink and Jeb dropped the pod into it.

'Now me beauties, you've seen how firm and weighty that house pod is?'

They chorused, 'Yes', respectfully.

'Now watch.' He turned on a big brass tap, water poured out and the house pod began to disintegrate. In seconds it was gone. Jeb wiped his hand on a towel and smiled. 'If we don't use that old house pod sharpish, then She will take it back quick as you like.'

'Why?'

He looked at Jonathan and pushed a large, gentle forefinger onto his nose. 'Because She needs that ol' stuff much more than we do. One of Her children in the making if you like.'

'But what does She do with it?'

'Make other things of course.'

'Where does the tap water come from?' interrupted William enthusiastically. He was really taken by all of this now. 'We get it from the well back home. Got to live in a town to have tap water.'

'That so?'

The boys nodded.

'Well, me loves, not here. She gives it to us from out of the ground.'

'Through pipes?'

William looked to Jon Bach, impressed with his quick thinking.

'No, Jonathan. Water and gas comes out of the ground and up into the walls when a new cottage has been fully grown. It is part of the house pods pattern - in the same way as the salmon knows that he must swim hard against the current to fulfil his life-work. This is because Mother Earth is behind every living thing and directs each one. The house pod is alive because it came from a living house.' He looked at their glowing faces. 'This ol' cottage is alive only in the sense that a plant is – not like a man or animal. Takes a good many months to grown a cottage of this size – maybe a year. When it is finished, a little pip remains where the water and gas will come out if the pip is broken. And so I connected up my brass tap in one place, the griddle in another, a shower in another.'

Silas took a turn. 'In the bigger villages in Ansaurius where things like taps, griddles, ovens, furniture and the like are made; people have to make things just like in your homeland, boys.' He took a little telescope from the squire's tail-coat pocket to illustrate his point by holding it up and turning it to and fro'. 'But in Ansaurius, people have learned to communicate with Mother Earth through special men and women, monks and nuns who lived long, long ago; so She knows what we require and the people know what is required of them. And what She requires of the people is most important. I want you both to understand that.

'This weary body that I inhabit is feeling fatigued. Let us all sit down.' He took off the tricorne hat, threw it on the table and they all joined him.

Jebridiah took out mugs for the two men and glasses for the boys from a cupboard, a leather flagon from another and as they sat back in their seats gently the ale was poured. The boys looked at Silas intently as he finished his large mug in one go, wiped his mouth, took a long breath and began.

'At first many people ignored what we now believe is the greatest truth humanity can ever understand if it is to survive. Now only the smallest of numbers question the truth of Mother Earth's existence.'

'Didn't God make the world, though?' William slurped his drink and stared back in challenge.

'Yes,' added Jonathan, 'and does this mean that Mother Earth is really God?'

Jeb was shaken by the mature questions until he very quickly realised that his friend, living temporarily within that creaking body and quaint old set of clothes, had power enough to open their young minds to mature reason – at least for the short time they were with him.

'God Himself is for each one of us to believe in or not. This choice we are all given. But after such a long time, the existence of Mother Earth as a living creature is all but unchallengeable in Ansaurius. Look around this living cottage if you doubt it. What She gives us is beyond question. If we destroy the Earth by selfishness and ignorance, what would God think of humanity destroying His wonderful creation? Many people say that God created the Earth as a living creature, as well as a planet, and us too. He created the whole universe. Others say that there is no God at all. If that is your thinking, anything can be considered, including the idea that the planet Earth is indeed God to humankind.'

'Do you believe in God, sir?' William had a deeply questioning look in his young face but there was a touch of mischief too.

'Ha! That's for me to know, young rascal, and you to find out what you believe.' He looked at Silas who was laughing gently.

Jebridiah refilled both mugs and glasses and then Silas took over the tale. 'Mother Earth gives many wondrous things to us but we must do a lot in return if we are to keep this world clean and healthy. And it is right to be that way. What would we become if everything was done for us? The man-made goods around us have been hard won with much energetic industry and they come here by way of markets and shops, just as it is back in your own home town, boys.'

Jebridiah then explained more as he wiped his bushy sideburns. 'Yes. I bought these furnishings years ago. I fitted this here griddle myself. The tap too. Do you want to see more, me beauties?'

And so the company toured the rest of the enchanting cottage. Each room was laid out most comfortably. Padded, well-made country furniture, easy chairs, book shelves for Jebridiah was a great reader as well as an accomplished carpenter. Flowers in little vases, shelves, tables chairs of all types and a big comfortable bed. There was no bath, but a shower; it was well made too, fitted by Jeb and connected, as he took great pains to point out, to the little pip where the shower head was supposed to be connected in the ceiling. A shower to William Williams was the most fantastic thing he had ever seen, he told Jeb and Silas this, and of his family's tin bath hung on the wall of their back kitchen, to which Jeb nodded respectfully.

Their time in Ansaurius had come to an end and the boys were instructed that they must leave soon. As Silas led them back up the hill, there was sadness at leaving the strange cottage and all gave a final wave to the Watchtaker, who was lighting a knobbly old clay pipe and he waved back merrily.

'I have brought you here today, Jonathan because Mother Earth has marked you out as a possible…'Silas paused, '…let us say She sees great things for you when you grow to be a man. 'And', he added looking at William, 'you are not to be left out of this. But I can say no more, only that everything you have been shown today will remain in your heads as an unconscious dream. You will remember nothing of it soon. This will help to bond you further – not that you two could be much firmer friends!' He smiled. 'This bonding will still be so when you grow up. You are both destined to come here again for great purpose. It is Her will. Do you understand?'

They both nodded easy acceptance as if every word made sense to them, which it did. Then the moment was passed and with it went all conscious memory of Silas' words - but the heart of his message which he had laid down so firmly was now set to return unclouded a long time in the future.

'Look up, boys! The faeries have returned.'

And so they had.

*     *     *

Not many moments later they stood between two fluted pillars, with a beautiful mosaic tiled floor beneath their feet. Fragments of time and reality which allowed their passage to Ansaurius, had now returned them to this world safely. Set on a stone table was the dark outline of a man's head with a peculiar halo of light behind it, which they recognised immediately. A large vault with mineral reflections glinted with faerie light, stone walls and the three rows of benches with darkened alcoves above looked down coldly. They were back in the cave temple of Mithras. The thrumming of the faerie host was muted, the boys looked around, but they could make out nothing except the sterling form of Squire Bellamy standing behind them.

'We are back home. At least near our homes. Do you know your way back to Hendre Bach from here, boys?'

They nodded together, dumbfounded in the faint light.

'I too am overwhelmed by all of this… Silas has gone you know.' The gentry squire stooped to his haunches. 'We shall always be friends now, you two and I. Is that not so?'

The boys nodded again.

'Do you know who Silas is?' questioned Jonathan.

'Jon Bach, don't ask such silly questions…' William interrupted sternly.

The ruffled sleeves shook as Bellamy cast away the reproach. 'No. No, me lads. I know what you mean, Jonathan. But I don't know *who* you mean – if you see what I mean!' For the first time they saw a huge smile on the aristocratic face and his gold tooth twinkled brightly. 'Something happens to me when he arrives, I become sleepy and I know no more. But whoever comes to me is good, that's all I know, boys. He will do us no harm, and, with luck he might do us a power of good as well.'

'We'd best be going now,' said William, 'It is getting late.'

'No. It'll be the same time as when we left, William. Don't you remember Silas said so.'

The Welsh boy nodded acknowledgement and they all moved slowly to the doorway in the portico. As the two turned to run off, they looked back to see Squire's happy face in the sunlight. He was crying copious tears of joy.

# Fourteen

Gwen Williams walked quickly into her farmhouse kitchen soon after nine o'clock the following morning with a half-wild tortoiseshell cat running around for food; on her arm was a woven lath trug full of fresh farm vegetables, on her brown weathered face a happy smile. Somehow the boys had returned quietly and continued their work with Taid. Gwen knew nothing of their escapade but a grandmother's instincts were being guardedly aroused. Three days had since passed uneventfully. She hurried across the flagstoned floor, rubber boots squeaking among the generous folds of a dark blue cotton dress flowing out around her ankles, then her eyes were smiling brightly at the fresh crop on the big deal kitchen table.

The trespasser-cat looked to its saucer of milk then ran fast, lapping up the contents quietly in seconds, as if never having seen food before, whilst runner beans, carrots and other choice specimens were sorted into neat piles. Ten minutes saw a black iron kettle steaming on its hook above her peat cooking fire and curling smoke rising into the stone chimney they called Jack Moog.

The Welsh country woman's small, almost petite size belied her strong personality. It had stamped itself around the place over many years, but today there was something more about her energetic doings; for an unmistakable, fiery resolve filled Gwen Williams like a fire. Small, nimble brown hands ran nervously about pins and a comb at the back of her head holding tightly pulled, flourishing silver hair in place, whilst astute hazel eyes held fixedly upon a letter laying on the table.

The letter had been taken out for the umpteenth time since arriving ten days ago, read and re-read to Owain, Nain and Taid Hafod, but to no one else. They had all deliberated at length. The two boys knew nothing of the matter, both camps in cautious careful silence of the other.

She sat down, staring hypnotically at the Central London postmark before picking up her tea and sipping it slowly, feeling awfully guilty at her own secrecy. Time for a decision. Events were now reaching a climax. She wanted to protect her ten-year-old English grandson as best she may. Jon Bach was settling in well at Hendre Bach. He had received two letters from Lord Webster, the only link with his old home life in Croydon. Although very defensive at first he showed them carefully, but trustingly to his new Nain. The contents were clearly from a kindly and loving man, but Gwen could sense something hidden under the words.

The boy knew, or would reveal no more. The recent demise of the Webster fortune had ended in near destitution for James and Siân, leaving Jonathan homeless and penniless. Gwen Williams found it hard to admit that her only daughter had abandoned Jon Bach and his aristocratic father to their Fate. This reality had almost broken the strong Welshwoman's heart, yet she kept it from everyone - even Owain - the depth of her pain was a very personal affair.

As Gwen sat with her thoughts that bright morning, musing on the sparse details she had gleaned about her son-in-law, she began to feel familiar tears of memory in her eyes. The Williams family had not been invited to Siân's high society wedding in London those eleven years before. Squire Bellamy, less eccentric then, had called her and Owain to one side on the way out from Church and showed them a picture of Siân and her new husband in the *London Gazette*. It had been pure chance that Bellamy had picked up the newspaper whilst at the London club of an associate. The Williams' knew nothing at all of their only daughter's marriage and could have died with shame. He gave them the paper as a souvenir.

James Webster's careful, almost bland recounting of flying experiences in his letters to Jonathan, the apologies for not being able to say more and vague promises to explain everything when he returned, seemed to support Jon Bach's ill-ease, as if his father was involved in at best, some strange venture or at worst, something ill-conceived and far away across the sea. Now another letter had arrived at their isolated little farm and its contents not only supported the ideas, but gave them another twist of intrigue.

Gwen looked at the first line of the address again, *Mr & Mrs Williams, family and Master Jonathan Webster,* then turned the envelope over and took out two sheets of deckle-edged writing paper. She read the words carefully as if all was new to her eye, following the most beautiful, flowing hand with ease.

*Savoy Hotel*
*Strand*
*London*

*17 July 1931*

*Dear Mr & Mrs Williams, your family and Jonathan*

*I hope you do not mind me writing out of the blue like this, I am an American friend of Lord James Webster, and wish to let you know he is well and doing fine in the United States. I have come on a sort of vacation to the British Isles and have asked the Rt. Hon. Eleanor Capenhurst (your aunt, Jonathan) for your address in Wales, so that I might make contact with you all.*

*I am pleased to say that James should be home in Gt. Britain very soon now, around the end of July to the beginning of August with any luck. We got to know each other when he was flying passenger airplanes from Chicago down to Indianapolis in Indiana. Do you remember, Jonathan, he told you a little of this in his first letter? I was with him when he wrote you. He is the most wonderful man and I'm sure you must all be very proud of him. My job then was what is now called a flight attendant in the States, that's a girl who looks after folks on flights, serving coffee and trying to keep them cheerful. James was my pilot.*

*I would like to say a lot more but I can't because James is flying a special airplane now and it has all got to remain a secret until he comes home. I expect he will be able to tell you much more then. My second reason for writing is to ask if I can bring him straight to your farm after he arrives in Europe, please? Can we leave that by saying I have made the connections! Jonathan must be dying to see his father and I know James is just dying to see him, as well as the rest of you, of course. Will this be OK, Mr & Mrs Williams? I need to know so that arrangements can be made in advance. I would like to say all of us who worked with James at the airline loved the guy. You are so lucky to have him. So I don't want you folks to worry any more than you've got to.*

*I am a country girl (in spite of this real dandy London address) and understand just how much work there is on a farm. But unfortunately we will probably have to arrive without warning I'm afraid, say between July 30 and August 5 as there will be no way of contacting you in time. If the dates change outside this I will write you again. Would you be so kind as to reply to me at the above address as soon as you can and confirm that we can come, please? As soon as I have your agreement, I will make all the necessary arrangements. I do hope this is OK and look forward to meeting with you all very soon.*

*My best wishes*

*Jane Levine*


Gwen folded the letter and returned it carefully to the envelope. She had thought immediately of Siân when it arrived because of the Savoy Hotel headed paper and had quickly turned to the last page for a signature before reading it through. Her heart had leapt wildly. Jane is the English translation of the name Siân and for one ecstatic moment she thought the letter was from her errant daughter who had somehow abandoned the Welsh name in a final attempt to rid herself of her past. It soon became clear that this was not the case.

If the writer was as much in love with Jonathan's father as her words seemed to imply - for any woman who had ever loved a man could only conclude this was the case - then Lady Siân Webster had almost certainly lost her nobleman husband for good, and she could hardly be surprised at that! Gwen Williams replied to Jane Levine the day her letter had arrived, an equally friendly one and one which offered a firm welcome to both her and James. That in itself revealed much of Gwen's fundamental decency and great personal strength, for by so doing, she had probably shut the door on her own daughter reclaiming a broken marriage. Yet proud as she was, Gwen was still willing to help complete strangers, a man and woman whom she had never met, for the sake of her grandson. She knew now to her shame that Siân had behaved appallingly.

As she sipped tea isolated parts of her family's history, both past and present, started to merge into one tangible whole. It seemed as if things were taking the path Fate had ordained and the opening element of it would start soon. This day, she decided, Jonathan would be told everything.

The Welsh are a very old race, their culture and language are among the oldest in Europe and it was said then among hill folk that a lifetime working on the land, generation after generation, awarded a sixth sense. Gwen Williams knew little of these things. Nor gave too much thought to them anyway. Yet she just could not get this son-in-law she had never met out of her mind.

She had just finished the cup of tea and began baking when William's normally loud voice sounded across the yard, thin snatches of encouragement said on the run. Jonathan came through the big black door fast running, his older cousin close behind. The pair almost knocked Gwen over.

His face was bloodless white and Gwen's shock froze for seconds on her face as she looked him up and down; worn shirt, short ragged trousers, long school socks and big lace up black boots - all hand-me-downs from William - string about his waist holding up the trousers, knees grazed. Normal attire and condition for a farm boy, except physically, he looked terrible.

'What ever's the matter, cariad?' Jon Bach stood panting, wordless for the moment, Gwen, her hands covered in flour from a mixing bowel lifted a single finger and smiled, 'Calm yourself.' His stare was deep and total into his grandmother's still beautiful eyes, begging for comfort and help.

'I feel really sick, Nainy.'

'Now come, come. Just stand there...'

Quickly washed hands were about him and Gwen's right hand felt his forehead then she drew him into her embrace.

'Go get Nain Hafod, quickly, William. Say Jon Bach's got a temperature.'

He made for the door.

'Say we will get him cleaned up and up to bed before she arrives. And...'

William swung back into the doorway.

'You help Nain Hafod all the way down here, you hear? And be good.'

William responded quickly and was away in a moment.

'Well, what a t'do and no mistake.' They cuddled and then she drew him back and tousled his shock of light brown hair. It was wringing wet, way beyond the warmth of the day. She scanned his face and felt his head again. 'Up to bed with you and take care on the stair. You've caught something an' no mistake, but Nain Hafod will make you better. I will come up in a minute with some tea until they get back.'

As Jonathan made for the stair, Megan, William's mam arrived at the back kitchen door having seen the boys come in and together the women helped Jon Bach into his tiny bed in the attic room. Sickness soon came on. Evening turned to night and with it another day. On her second visit, Nain Hafod produced medicines, herbs and balms, some to be administered now, others later if he didn't get better. The family decided to pool together what money they could find which was very little for Doctor Morgan to come up from Llanrwst if Jonathan was no better soon. Nain Hafod's pride and clear concern for the boy had her out picking plants secretly in Squires Wood and working late into the night at pestle and mortar making potions for the next day. Bur nothing seemed to work. The boy neither rallied nor fell further into the fever's abyss.

Horse and rider crested Moel Seisnog like a sudden apparition leaping out of fireside tales, thunder from the hooves the only sound above a rising wind. The man could ride of that there was no doubt, and a glance showed his great white horse to be a well bred animal, powerful and brave as it skirted boulder, shale spill from the white broken cliff and gorse bushes that led to Nain and Taid Hafod's isolated little cottage. Dusk would soon be giving way to night and a welcome glow lit the diamond-paned windows with a gentle, candled yellow.

The horse leapt the slate boundary marker and in seconds had halted to whinny and thud of biting hooves near the cottage's black front door, almost invisible in the gloom. Behind the sturdy door stood old Elias Jones hard against it with his double-barrelled shotgun, loaded and cocked.

'My God. It is Mad Silas.' His wife, Morfydd's clear husky voice had fear written there, but like her husband, she still had the spirit of a lion in spite of being over eighty. 'I've never seen him out in the open before - ever...' she moved quickly from the window and stood close beside Elias, '...only in the forests and wild places where no one else goes but us.'

'Why is that madman outside our door then?' His Welsh words had anger in them now and he felt his wife's calming hand on his arm.

'Elias. He has got his blunderbuss gun with him...'

Watery blue eyes twinkled resolve. 'And I've got old Meg,' he patted the stock of his twelve bore.

A voice, strong and confident rang out beyond the door, calling their names and asking if they would open the door. The words were in Welsh but had cultured English threaded through by accent.

Slowly Elias opened the door and lifted the shotgun, Morfydd right behind looking over his shoulder. Just as she had warned, there sat Old Mad Silas, the blunderbuss fortunately resting at ease on his lap and a white hand, diamond rings aglitter, patting the horse's neck. Formally, he touched the edge of his black velvet tricorne hat edged with gold, the horse restless and blowing through flared nostrils whinnied. Silas' powdered hair lifted in wisps about the red tail-coat, face powder to his cheeks, the white muslin cravat at his throat all gave the wild figure an air of danger. A madman at your door.

'I bid thee both good eveningtide.'

Taid was always at pains to be polite with gentry, knowing what he thought was his place and that this must be Squire Bellamy sat before him, in spite of everything to the contrary. Every other sense though was saying shut the door, push the bolt and be quick about it.

'Good evening.' Morfydd's voice from behind came before Elias could answer. 'What would you be wanting at this late hour, sir?'

'This is the dwelling abode of Elias and Morfydd Jones?'

'And if it is?' Taid's voice raised a little now.

The white horse became jittery, Silas brought it back by reining well, but more by using a firm voice.

'Gad, sir. We wish you no harm. I know you both...'

'You do,' croaked Taid, struggling to clear his throat.

'Indeed. I come here from my duties fain to speak about your great grandson, the English orphan called Jonathan.'

Morfydd suddenly pushed Elias to one side. 'What about him?' Her eyes were ablaze, fear in her old heart. 'Is he alright? If the boy's hurt...'

Silas raised his gentry hand, a bright moon had drifted from silvered clouds behind the apparition, polished buckled shoes at the stirrups glistening with the soft rays. 'Hush, Madam. That orphan is as my liegeman, and I as his liege lord. I would ne'r hurt him or his kin and kind for anything. But I do know the terrible fever that besets the boy and I fain ride to you this dark night to give you a small, valuable quantity of silver salix to cure him. It is a powerful draught when infused in brandy. My word upon it...'

'How do you know him to be ill?' Morfydd spoke pure Welsh now.

'I know many things.' His words remained English. Rheumy eyes misted more. And then Silas pulled on the reins turning the horse carefully. He fumbled in a braided flap pocket of his tail-coat and pulled out a fine leather bag, tooled in gold, and bound with golden drawstring. He threw it to Elias who caught it deftly.

'Thrice daily, a full thimble measure of silver salix infused in brandy – watered brandy as he is still a boy – then it and good care will drive the fever from his heart.'

The cottagers nodded. That was the only reply they could make, and with a rush Old Mad Silas shot out across the small, dark parcel of land, clearing the slate boundary markers with ease and was quickly swallowed by the night. Only the thunder of Butterscotches hooves hung long on the chilly night air as the couple stood there shaken at their homely old door.

It was a week later that their Jon Bach, William at his bedside almost every minute he could be spared, began to rally.

## Fifteen

The first Saturday in August arrived warm and well. Jonathan was outside for the first time, still in pyjamas, William's hand-me-downs, wrapped in a shawl and seated on an old wicker chair. In his weakened state the story of how Nainy Hafod had come by silver salix still haunted him. Nature was at her most radiant, birds sung their joy at being alive, bees hummed, swallows darted the clear blue heavens and the height of summer burnished all creation as if it could be burnished no more. The views across to the Ladies of Snowdon were spectacular then, even for August - one of those rare days when a heat haze in summer had not risen to soften the view at all, for everything was still sharp and crisp as could be.

Soon after he was settled in his wicker chair, Gwen carefully showed him the surprising letter from the American lady. Another wild surprise to be digested. They talked about her words and - in gentle terms at least - what they implied. The boy then remained thoughtful for some hours, mostly alone, for everyone was busy particularly at that time.

It was late morning when Owain turned the corner at the end of the farmhouse carrying a chair from the back kitchen. Jonathan lifted from half-sleep as his grandfather sat beside him; the strong, wiry frame clad in a worn shirt, unseen tattered sleeves rolled up, corduroy trousers tied at the bottoms above hob-nailed boots. His big leather face creased with a smile of joy at what he saw. 'The good Lord be praised. You look a lot better than you did yesterday, Jon Bach. Duw, me thinks you're on the mend at last!' Owain was still in his prime. Slower than thirty years ago, but slow in that easy sense now, where a man knows his way around his own world, and has come to terms with the ways of other worlds beyond his ken. It was true that Jon Bach had only just begun to rally. This was perhaps not the best time to talk of serious things which might cause alarm but the countryman's instincts said otherwise and mostly he followed what he felt.

Jonathan turned in the chair, his mother's eyes smiling, colour in his cheeks for the first time in days. 'Light your pipe up, please, Taid. I like to see you smoke your pipe.'

The hill farmer nodded. 'Good idea, boy. I want to talk some men's talk with you if you're up to it. Just you and me. OK, Jon Bach?' He lifted an eye from beneath silvered brows.

Owain Williams was a quiet and resourceful man, more maybe than this tale has so far revealed. Never wholly put upon by life, Owain was always there, taking on life's burdens that would overwhelm many.

Simple in his tastes and unpretentious in manner - even for a plain hill man - he had, as seen through an English eye at least, the superficial appearance of a typical yeoman. But his mind was always roaming, holding an infinite capacity for mastering detail. Larger issues, politics and the things of city were beyond him. He had no access to such and was open and honest of the fact. Yet great moral courage and an inveterate obstinacy were built into Owain Williams, like mortar into a castle. No one, not even Gwen, knew of his secret and from where such strength of character had actually sprung.

The Welshman sat back in his chair, lit his pipe and the blue smoke lifted and wreathed around him. With care he started upon words that were not easy, attending to deep feelings for what he was about to say. 'We are Welsh folk here. Celtic blood in us. An ancient breed and no mistake.'

He looked firmly across, Jonathan was, as usual, hanging onto his every word - at least when a story was being told.

'I was the same age as William when I had a dream...' Owain pulled on his pipe, looking straight ahead into the bright day as if acting out a part that had been practised for many years. 'A lady walked with me in a green meadow. She told me the blood in my veins runs back through time to great peoples who lived here long, long ago. She said my blood was their blood and even though my birth and upbringing here are of the humblest kind, in me is the building blocks of noble and ancient men.'

'Ancient men?'

Owain gazed fixedly at the figure of his English grandson wrapped in the shawl, face full of wonder, a child whom he had come to love so dearly. 'Aye.'

'Who were they?' Something prickled in his mind, but he didn't know what.

'That I don't know. But the lady said I would live long and one day my bloodline will be mixed with another through marriage, a powerful blood from an ancient people like mine who go back far. And because of the blood mix, that person will receive great gifts of knowing.'

Jonathan was full awake now. No concern on his young face. Only conviction. 'Was the lady's name, Deldramena?'

'Why do you ask that, boy?'

'Because a lady came to me in the night whilst I was asleep, weeks and weeks ago now. Her name was Deldramena and afterwards, on other nights I saw my mother first and then my father...'

The two stared at each other, eyes wide in astonishment yet oddly full of a sudden, powerful recognition.

'I was there with them, Taid. Honest I was. I walked about. No one could see or hear me. But I could see them, hear them all and so much more. And at first I was scared.'

'And now?'

'No. Not now.'

Owain raked the top of his pipe with a brown finger, thoughts still his own. 'Have you told anyone else about this apart from Nainy Hafod, Jon Bach?' Wise eyes were guarded.

The boy stared silently at his grandfather from the wicker chair.

'Well?'

The stare continued for a while and then he looked towards the Ladies. 'Only William, Taid.'

'Who said...'

'That I had been dreaming and that if I didn't get a move on Nain would hit me with dobio.'

Owain laughed. A full, hearty laugh as he often laughed when happy, when they were walking to Church, or driving the cart down from the Hafod full of peat pulled by Prince and the boys or Gwen singing songs with him on the evening air. Now, suddenly he was very happy.

*    *    *

Jon Bach had slept most of the afternoon. He awoke to a lot of talking coming from the yard on the other side of the house. The walls of the old stone farmhouse were stout and all he could grasp were many faint voices, seemingly talking at once. He did feel better now, got out of his wicker chair, wrapped the shawl about himself and followed the little flagstoned path around the house to the yard.

The sight that greeted him was wonderful. Standing outside the kitchen door were his father and a beautiful lady surrounded by the whole family. Nain and Taid Hafod were dressed in Sunday best clothes, Megan, William's mam looked really lovely with her best dress and hat, Nain and Taid were all especially spruce, even William looked different, he had combed his hair, or had had it combed. Somehow a telephone message had come through to the post office in Llanrwst to say that Lord James Webster would be arriving at Hendre Bach late afternoon. Maldwyn Hughes borrowed Dafydd Post's bicycle and had peddled the six miles at break neck speed to warn the family. Jonathan just stood at the end of the farmhouse staring in disbelief for long seconds.

'Look! Jon Bach.' William pointed. Everyone stopped talking and turned. Jonathan ran full pelt towards his dad. The shawl came off revealing repaired pyjamas above big black lace up boots clunking the flags and then scrunching across the gravel at an ever increasing pace until, with that same confidence that only ten years and a strong dad confers, Jon Bach launched himself at James in utter joy at their meeting. A cheer went up. Mutual shouts and shrieks of glee as father and son whirled around. The big black boots went straight out in the breeze, James leaning backwards for his only son had grown more than he had ever realised.

Then Jonathan pulled himself tight to his father's broad chest as if never again would he ever let him go. He felt a strong hand in his hair and felt warm tears on his cheek.

Suddenly, through an opened eye William was at his side. 'Don't worry about crying. You can do that when it's your dad!'

'I'm not crying...' He knew he was though, pulled back the tears and looked up into his father's strong face. And it came back. Everything. All that he knew and loved in that smile, those dark twinkling eyes, and the definite masculine smell which only a time like this really brings to mind.

They all trooped into the house. Taid Hafod taking off his bowler hat and his still sprightly wife admonishing him for not keeping Church boots clean, William running around the big deal table shouting, Pero and Moss barking and getting in everyone's way and Gwen asking who wanted tea. Taid was shaking James' hand and telling what an extraordinary son he had, Megan brought out a large fruit cake from the pantry which was kept only for Christmas and very special occasions. The big black iron kettle on its hook above the peat fire was soon steaming merrily, bread was cut, sandwiches circulated, milk for the boys, tea for the rest. Everyone all around the table eating, drinking, talking and laughing.

Jonathan, mouth full of cake looked across to see the American lady smiling at him. 'Are you feeling better?' Her voice was smooth, like lovely silk.

He nodded. 'I read your letter. Nain showed me.' He stopped chewing and stared hard. 'Do you love my dad?'

She gave only the slightest flush of embarrassment. Jonathan saw it but carried on determinedly. 'Do you?'

Everyone was talking and laughing around them. She slid her chair nearer. 'That matters doesn't it.'

'My mother's gone...and I still love her...I do. '

138

Jane Levine's blue eyes glinted from the sunlight filtering through the tiny window above his head.

He could see they were wet.

'And you think I want to take her place?'

More cake filled his mouth and he felt himself suddenly very tearful indeed, wanting to run to James. 'Well, aren't you?' The words were challenging, muddled with food.

Before she could answer, Megan offered more tea or milk and came between them to fill their mugs.

'Your first question was do I love your father? The answer is, yes I do; very, very much. The answer to your second question is, no I do not want to take your mother's place. I could never do that.'

The boy looked hard at her again. She was wearing a summer dress with blue flowers on it and a little hat that set her face off nicely. She had lipstick on. She was very beautiful. American ladies wore lipstick. Jonathan knew that and it didn't make her cheap. He had thought about this lady and her letter a lot. He also thought that he might like her one day. Perhaps. But he loved his mother - in spite of what she had done to him and his father. Jane smiled and Jon Bach smiled back.

His attention was suddenly taken by William who was asking if James really had flown a plane all the way across the ocean from America.

'Have you, Dad - really and truly?' he called out across the table - boyhood grasp taking temporary mastery over his now deep spiritual senses.

They all turned, Jonathan walked around the table to James' beckon and sat on his father's knee. William not wanting to be outdone squeezed onto the kitchen stool that Nain Hafod was sitting on, so that he was right there next to James. Both boys now looked up full of expectation for a real story.

'Yes I have. Not on my own you understand, I had a crew with me and passengers.'

'Passengers? Wow.' The latter word, drawn out by both lads made for some laughter.

James paused, gathering thoughts and the ticking of the grandfather clock in the corner suddenly made its presence felt, pulling them all together within that old family room in a few airy seconds. Everyone there felt kinship, children and adults alike; finalising an ancient enactment somehow, completing a circle at long last made whole.

Owain and Gwen had also been thinking of their daughter, Siân. Wondering how she must be now and how sad it was that she could not have stayed married to this man and been there with them all. Gwen looked at James in those few seconds before he began his story; his dark, passionate eyes, long handsome face, open persona filling her heart, heard his deep English voice in her mind, its cadence and its diction, the strength and decency there, the prominent cheekbones under a brown sun-tanned skin and she felt her emotions running away. And yet if he had been plain as plain looking could be, at that moment she would have still loved him.

The story of how the great flying boat had lost power more than one thousand miles out from Newfoundland and had to be brought down on the open sea sounded like a miracle to the boys - indeed to them all. A calm before the storm James called it. Flying boats are designed to land and take off from estuary waters, or still waters he told them. Never on the open sea, even in good weather - for a machine as vulnerable to impact as this would break up in an instant.

He stressed how unusually calm the sea had been at the moment of decision to take her down. They had never seen the like of it before. Repairs were made quickly as Condor rested there, as if on a mill pond, and soon she lifted off into what became a terrible storm.

Jonathan remembered Deldramena in his dream and holding her hand as they had watched two flying machines cross the wide sky together. One real, the other a spiritual guide she said. She told him the silver one was piloted by Davy Mack, his father's friend whilst safely in that in between time before passing on to his Maker. A new fighter plane on test had crashed the day before in England and Davy was killed. Under the circumstances Jon Bach had decided that it was best not tell William any more about Deldramena.

Jane, ready for the arrival of Condor, had arranged for a small aeroplane to be at their disposal. James flew it across to Caernarfon airfield in N. Wales the following day and then they travelled on to Hendre Bach by motorcar. Everyone was thrilled by the tale, chatter rose once more, they continued with tea, sandwiches, milk and more fruit cake. Even the two dogs seemed to have had their fill.

What James didn't know was that his only son was far more special than he could possibly dream, as every bit as special as his Welsh Taid had genuinely portrayed him when James and Jane had first arrived. The blending of two ancient bloodlines had indeed opened a door beyond all their understandings. It would be later in the boy's life when the enchantment now coursing his veins would be turned into a remarkable reality.

Jon Bach stayed happily with the Williams' for two more weeks until his father could set up temporary home back in Croydon. From there, Jonathan was reunited with his old friends and returned to school. Jonathan and William became life long friends, not only because of these shared experiences, but because of future times as yet to be fulfilled.

Jonathan never saw his mother again. It was believed that Siân was killed in Rome in the Second World War at the time of the Allied invasion.

To read more about Ansaurius and what lies there, look out for DOORKEEPER TWO.

Friends of my work call it Octavism. The belief that the Earth is not only alive, but aware and we ignore Her needs at our peril - the Gaia Theory but with a soul.

Printed in the United Kingdom by
Lightning Source UK Ltd., Milton Keynes
138199UK00002B/151/P